THE AFTER EDEN SERIES

PURE CONSPIRACY

A Select Novel

AUSTIN DRAGON

Published by Well-Tailored Books, California

Pure Conspiracy / The After Eden Series

978-0-9967060-1-8 (hardcover)
978-0-9967060-0-1 (paperback)
978-0-9909315-9-1 (ebook)

http://www.austindragon.com

Book cover design by Leslie K.
Formatting by Polgarus Studio

Printed in the United States of America

FIVE STAR REVIEWS ABOUT THE AFTER EDEN SERIES!

A heart racing thriller!

"This futuristic thriller will grab you and take you on an emotional, spiritual, and political ride that you won't forget. I loved it!"

An Eerie Thought of What is to Come

"This sci-fi, futuristic Tek world is an eerie thought of what is to come. Surveillance drones hovering overhead 24/7. A.I. in our homes, our ears, everywhere we look. No more pets, how about a robo-dog?...I'm definitely looking forward to book two of this series!"

Captivating

"Austin Dragon has created a book that will not only captivate its reader from the very first sentence, it will not let go until the very last word and leave you eagerly awaiting more. Thy Kingdom Fall has all the elements to make a perfect story that includes so many aspects all over the spectrum of genres that includes thriller, science fiction, religion, politics, and so much more. A. Dragon's writing style will go under my classification as one of the top 10 authors I've read."

World of tomorrow today!

"When I read the description of this book I had to give it a read. What's not to like politics, thriller, action adventure, intrigue, and imminent war on the horizon...The author has made the technology believable as it will probably be in the future. The author has put together a very amazing world with vividly portrayed characters."

Overflowing with intrigue

"Deft political maneuvers, abolishment of religion as we know it, and a growing dependency on technology fuse together to create a sprawling plot that completely sucked me in from page one. Political leaders are so well-written that I was able to actually see them and hear their speeches. The reference to the Three Towers was especially lifelike and chilling. The book handles religion so wildly that I'm not sure it's ever been done quite like this. It feels very current as you move through the book, even though it's futuristic...A page-turner for certain - you won't be disappointed. I will be purchasing the complete series as quickly as the author completes them.

The Future is No Garden of Eden

"The future is no Garden of Eden, and Austin Dragon writes a sharp, realistic picture of just what to possibly expect. As a vivid techno-thriller, drones and computers watch and monitor everything in our futuristic world. But the real test is whether they will be enough to help stop World War III."

What's Not to Like?

"When I read the description of this book I had to give it a read. What's not to like: politics, thriller, action adventure, intrigue, and imminent war on the horizon...It's a world where technology rules the world."

Pure Conspiracy

By Austin Dragon

A Select Novel in the AFTER EDEN futuristic thriller series

Pure Conspiracy

The After Eden Series (The Genesis of World War III)

This is how the End began.

Every era has its conflicts between opposing factions—a war between ideologies or cultures; sometimes it goes no further than words; but other times, it goes far beyond.

Race and ethnicity are no more. Class and nationalism remain. But above all—even more than the rift between those who dwell in the shiny, A.I.-controlled, Grid-monitored tek-cities of the masses and those that prefer to live in the territories beyond—is between the irreligious super-majority and the religious minority.

It all happened simply, slowly, legally, "logically," one step after another, then more significant and more provocative, ending in ways most would never have imagined—a transformation of things that some would call Heaven, and others, Hell.

In all things there is a moment when the path to an outcome becomes inevitable, irreversible—here, they are revelations of *pure conspiracy*.

Welcome to the world—four years away from the 22nd century!

"After Eden, Thy Kingdom Fall.
All Kingdoms Fall, New Kingdoms Rise."

"America isn't one nation, it's two."
– Kristiana Price, future elder of the Amish Order, 2088

"I want a *solution of finality* to these Jew-Christians.
What's that word they have?—Amen."
– President T. Wilson of the United States, 2089 (third term)

Net-Dictionary

Wolf 359

1. A red dwarf star located in the Leo constellation, approximately 7.8 light-years from Earth, making it one of the stars nearest to our solar system.

2. A fictional space battle in the Star Trek Universe between the United Federation of Planets and the Borg Collective in the year 2367.

3. The opening battle of World War III in New York City on September 11, 2125. Over sixty percent of the United States of America Atlantic Oceanic Battle Fleet was destroyed by the Supreme Islamic Caliphate Battle Group on the first day.

Other terms:

Pagan: (universal or American usage) a non-believer of god or gods; one that doesn't believe in religion, often negative to, hostile to, or hateful of religion.

Jew-Christian: (American usage [by non-religious people]) a religious person, other than Muslim.

Faither: (global usage [by religious people]) a religious person, other than Muslim.

Tek World: common slang for tek-cities, tek-metropolises, or general tek-society.

Resistance: (pre-World War III)

1. [by non-religious people] government term for the network of Jew-Christian domestic "terrorists" in America.

2. [by religious people] the civilian resistance force against the militant, anti-religious American government.

Continuum:

1. (general usage) the parallel society created by and controlled exclusively by Faithers outside of Tek World.

2. (formal usage) the formal alliance of the New Protestant Order, New Jewish Continuum, New Catholic Order, Mormon Order, the African Collective, Shogun, and the Magi.

Table of Contents

The following story takes place *after* the events of

Rising Leviathan (After Eden Series, Book #3)

and *before* the events of

Red Halo (After Eden Series, Book #4)

Death of the Red Hat Man

**The Pacific Ocean, Russia, The Russian Bloc (Greater Russia
and Eastern Europe)
8: 57 a.m., 21 August 2096**

The neon-ivory, American cruise liner sails the calm waters with
the tek-cities of Greater Russia in the distance. On the main deck,
the private party of senior male American executives continues—
techno music blaring, wait staff serving plenty of glasses of liquid
drugs, scantily-clad sex workers hanging on the arms of the
polyamorous male passengers, and the captain moving about,
socializing.

At 9:00 a.m. the sky is consumed by a flash. Everyone's
personal e-pad, tablet, Net-interface glasses, and device stops. The
ship's lights, power, machines, and systems stop. The entire sky
rumbles as if a bolt of lightning came from outer space itself.
Everyone looks around. People on the deck and the port windows
watch it grow in the distance, many miles away—a yellowish
mushroom cloud, unimaginable in size, expands and rises higher
into the sky, filling their entire view.

The captain watches in horror. He can already see the ocean

waters move away—the coming tidal wave is going to be beyond comprehension.

Smack! Something hits the deck only a couple of feet from him. He looks up and sees more. Birds, real and surveillance bots made to look like birds, fall from the sky, all around for as far as the eye can see.

"Abandon ship! Get everyone to the escape pods!" he yells to crew.

His eyes look out to the ocean horizon and he sees a wall of water rising. He whispers to himself, "We'll never make it."

He glances up again. So massive, so high, so monstrous—the yellowish, mega-mushroom cloud hangs frozen in the sky, above the "big blue."

Wastelands, South Carolina
2:02 a.m., 20 October 2096

The Wastelands. Trog-land. Beyond the metropolises are endless miles of empty deserts of sand and rock, bleak plains, bare forests, and ever-blowing dust. The civilized do not live here. People say, "Only savage humans and feral animals do." Some also say unnatural creatures. The solitude is interrupted by a convoy of land-hovering transports zipping along the surface so fast that the dirt and dust do not even have time to react to create a trail.

Yonah stares out the porthole windows through thick, tinted, night-vision goggles, though the outside passes by so fast that he cannot make out a thing. He is outfitted in a flight suit and fitted helmet with an air regulator mask covering the lower half of his face. He sees why he was instructed to keep the eyewear on when he first climbed into the 'catamaran'—a super-sonic-capable hover-transport vehicle, with each of its ten passengers sitting in pods, one in front of the other, single file. The blinding flashes in the night of sand lightning. They look like a natural occurrence but are actually one of the many man-made defenses created by Faithers to protect their territory. Sand lightning, emanating from the ground, can strike and down a sky-ship or drone thousands of feet in the air, and they can strike and explode any approaching land-based vehicle. Besides the flashes that illuminate the complete blackness of the night, he also sees dots of light along the horizon in the far distance—the only marks of civilization in the wasteland. They are either nearby Trog-land settlements or Outland suburbs or distant mega tek-cities.

It will take a couple of hours for the ten-vehicle convoy to arrive at their Jewish enclave destination—one of the larger Faither cities of the South. This is how they travel—in the dark of night, quickly, quietly, and in convoy. The threats are numerous, but sat-recon tracking and active drone interceptors, both controlled by the Grid-government, are what they worry about most. Fortunately for Faith World, in the current political climate, the Pagans are busy fighting amongst themselves—the tek-city elite versus Outland and Trog-land sub-populations.

But political climates never remain the same.

Masada Enclave, New Georgetown, South Carolina
7:38 a.m., 21 October 2096

The conference room was made to accommodate thirty people comfortably, but more than double that capacity crowd inside. From their styles of dress—business casual, traditional black, or traditional colors, most with head coverings of kippah, knit caps, or kufi—the men are of the Conservative, Orthodox, or Judeo-Spanish Jewish Orders. Some of the men sit Indian style on the single heavy oval table in the center. Their attention is focused on the main vid-screen at the front of the room. The large face of a man looks back at them with short black hair, a full beard, and a mustache with flecks of gray throughout.

"We cannot proceed with this!" a man yells. "We have Russians dropping bombs and their government is in the process of purging their religious citizens just like the American government tried to do here to us two decades ago. And the CHINs did a long time ago to theirs."

"Religious people in the Russian Bloc aren't exactly the same as us," another man interjects. "We call our Pagans here 'Pagans,' but they're atheists. Over there they really are pagans. Witches, Druids, Satanists, and so many others that they call Old World religions."

"Yes, but what we're talking about is having collaborators, here, in our midst, again. To purposely create a dangerous security situation for ourselves within the Community again. Why?"

"Especially with all that we went through, including violent civil war, three of them, to rid ourselves of quisling spies," a rabbi adds from the side of the room.

"And we still don't know what happened to the Orthodox Christians in Russia," another man in the back says—Mr. Tova.

"And they had Behemoth," a man next to him says—Rabbi Henriques.

"Exactly," the man continues. "Why are we doing this, Mr. Elliott? Why are the Conservatives pushing this?"

The man on the vid-screen holds back a laugh. "Mr. Ira, I can assure you, and you have colleagues there who will back me up, that the Conservatives are not pushing this. If a vote were held today within the Conservative Jewish Order, this plan would be dead on arrival. It is solely the efforts of a few, no more. I have been asked to take the lead, because of similar work I've done over the years within our Community after our civil wars, and with the Christians and others. This is just a conversation, nothing more.

No one, including me, has committed to anything."

"Conversations always lead to something," the man challenges.

"I can assure you that is not the case here," Elliott answers back.

"Shouldn't we table this until after the full Continuum meeting, in light of these Russian Bloc incidents?" another man asks.

"We can, but I say we push ahead and resolve it now, one way or the other. I don't like to postpone headaches for later. Get it over with now. Gentlemen, I understand the difficulty here."

"Elliott, we have no issues with talking to Lot Jews, or any Faithers. Those hiding in the tek-cities out of safety are one thing, but the Exiles? Excommunication must mean something or it means nothing. They were excommunicated for plotting and collaborating with the government and President 'Haman' against us—their own people."

"This is the exact kind of behavior that led to the Fall of Jewish Israel with its government. Negotiating with our enemies and collaborators," a large Orthodox man says from the front row, eliciting nods of agreement.

"Gentlemen, let's not engage in revisionist history," Elliott says. "Like Western Europe, it wasn't talk that led to Israel's fall; it was their actions, or lack of action. For us, we excommunicated most of the Exiles more than twenty years ago. Should the excommunication be extended to their children and grandchildren who were not even born yet?"

"Yes!" men shout out.

"That is a trick concocted by the Exiles to circumvent their excommunication and we will not allow it," a man yells.

"That's not what it is," Elliott counters. "Gentlemen, we are Jews, and is not forgiveness part of our mandate as Torah believers? We have to have the conversation. We did so with the Orthodox and the Hasidim after our civil wars."

"That was different," a man counters.

A man stands up in the back—Rabbi Oren. "Since the Orthodox Jewish Order's name is being brought up in vain"—men chuckle—"may I weigh in on the issue? I echo Elliott's assessment that the conversation should at least happen, and you know I am no pushover when it comes to these matters. Half of you in this room were too small to remember when there was the invisible rift within the Orthodox. If not for simple conversations, there would have been no—to use a Christian term—*reformation* within the Orthodox. As a young man, I was frequently at odds with old Ultra-Orthodox ways. It seemed unseemly to me—reading the Torah all day. You honor Yahweh by reading and *living* His Word, not reading it all day and shirking away your responsibilities as a man and having your women raise the children *and* do all the work, literally, which also included, doing the fighting for our very survival against the Pagans here in America, and the same in Russian Bloc and CHIN territories, and the Muslims in Western Europe and Jewish Israel. We had to be equal partners with our brothers in Judaism and not invisible bystanders. I stand before you as a man who was threatened with expulsion myself—*Oren the Troublemaker* is what I was called. We had to change, so we had our little, bloodless reformation. Orthodox won out over Ultra-Orthodox. We don't even use the word Ultra-Orthodox anymore. The Hasidim did the same within their Order, though there was some violence. The point is, the Orthodox people were made better and the Jewish people were made better by our continued inclusion within the Community. It was all made possible by the willingness to have a simple conversation.

"That is also why we now have the Jewish Continuum—the union of all our Jewish Orders. My own obstinacy and, yes, even my own pride, initially stood in the way of what we all universally recognize as the greatest alliance Jews have ever had in our history. The only thing worse than a mind open to everything is a mind closed to everything."

The room is calmed by his words.

"Oren, the Martin Luther of Orthodox!" a man calls out, which starts some laughter in the room.

"What is this conversation going to lead to?" the man asks more respectfully.

"Nothing that we don't want," Elliott answers. "We will not rush things and we will never ignore what the Exiles did. I say we handle the issue of Lot Jews and Hidden Ones separately from the Exiles."

The men in the room nod and respond with yeses.

"I have also consulted with the Shogun about this matter since they have had to deal with this type of issue more recently. I believe the bigger obstacle with the Exiles is not so much their past collaboration, but the fact that they are Jews in name only. Their religiosity is marginal at best, which by itself is not a problem, but it's often coupled with a hostility to those who are. Assimilation for them would be difficult enough with the feelings the Community has towards them, but with their attitudes, any real success becomes almost impossible. Atheist Western Europe allowed a separate, militant Muslim Western Europe in their precincts for more than half a century, and it destroyed them in the end. Distinctions and debates are welcome, but a people must be united. There's much to sort through and evaluate, but again, nothing is settled. I can't emphasize it enough—these series of conversations have a strong possibility of going nowhere, but we have to be open. If I had to pick between leaving them out there and having them reunited with us, I would choose the latter. If only for the sake of the children and to deprive the Pagans from having more of our people to meddle with."

"Gentlemen," Mr. Tova calls out with his booming voice, "we are running over as far as time and we have another meeting coming up. Is the group satisfied with the course of action to be taken?"

Men look at each other, but there are no objections.

"Is the Conservative Jewish Order formally in charge of this project?" another man asks.

"No, the Shamar Order is," Elliott answers. "I am just taking lead in the initial conversations and meetings. If it were to move to the next step, I would contract with members of the Shogun Order in the vetting process. However, before that, we would ask for formal approval by the full Jewish Continuum rather than only the executive board. This is too sensitive a matter. We either all agree to move forward or we don't do it at all."

Men in the room nod in agreement.

Mr. Tova looks around the room for any more discussion. "The meeting is adjourned, gentlemen."

As the men file out of the room, Rabbi Henriques asks Rabbi Oren, "Has Yonah arrived?"

Oren nods. "Early this morning. Hopefully, he managed to get at least a good couple hours of sleep."

Masada Enclave, New Georgetown, South Carolina
10:12 a.m., 21 October 2096

Yonah takes in the view from his window. Masada Enclave—a self-sufficient, self-contained, Jewish city of nearly one hundred and fifty thousand, populated by Orthodox, Conservatives, Hasidim, Judeo-Spanish, Arab, Persian, and a smaller community of Goth Jews. Many miles of open wasteland surrounds them, and the closest

Pagan tek-city is hundreds of miles away. Passage to and from any enclave is always dangerous. But once inside its thirteen-foot walls, it is deceptively non-tek, looking like quaint *shtetals*—the Yiddish word and universal colloquial for any "nice, little Jewish town," which nowadays is a full-fledged city. Their defense systems—from the invisible tek-jammer defense dome to retractable laser turrets and launchers on the wall to robotic drones and sentries strategically hidden throughout the city—are state-of-the-art and deadly. The perimeter of the wasteland leading to the enclave is also mined and booby-trapped with miniature killing robots.

Yonah's work takes him into the tek-cities often, but many Jews never leave their enclave. Maybe they will venture out to visit family and friends in another enclave. Some may even take a vacation to a Christian enclave—just to see. Amish and Mennonite ones are popular. The more adventurous may go visiting in the Catholic-held cities in Northern Mexico, Christian-controlled Africa (the African Collective), or the islands of the Shogun Christian in Japan. Beyond that, there is no other outside world.

They had his single room reserved at the main guest hotel not far from the wall. Yonah declined the offer of a late night meal from the proprietor. All he wanted was sleep in a warm bed and he did so as soon as he got to his room—the door opening automatically as it read his biometrics and closed after him—and his head hit the pillow.

The morning sun was all that it took to wake him ahead of his wristband alarm. From his three-story window, he could survey the city for many miles around. Farming towers were the farthest away—always shrouded in man-made clouds for security reasons. They are football-stadium-sized structures with gigantic multiple levels where the enclave grew its fruits and vegetables for its population and for outside sale. The crops are maintained, watered, and monitored by a full network of agro-bots, but primary farming is always done by humans. "You can use machines as long as you never forget how to do the work without them," he said to his own children to break them out of their anti-machine, "machines are the Devil" phase. There are also the sounds of people below.

He thoroughly enjoys the casual walk through the busy, almost cosmopolitan streets of the enclave. He hears mostly Hebrew, but there are conversations in Russian, Spanish, some German, some French, Arabic, and Persian. English remains the international language. Orthodox Jewish men, like him, are dressed all in black—long buttoned coats, shoes, pants, and kippot on their heads, but he wears a flat black cowboy hat instead. All Orthodox men have full beards and mustaches, as does he—his bushy black beard and mustache are going gray. Orthodox Jewish women wear plain clothes, covering from neckline to knee, modest tops, not too bright, and dark-colored skirts. Married women wear hats or wigs; single women do not. Conservative Jews dress more modern—suit and tie, or business casual; men often wear kippot in public. Arab and Persian Jews like bright colors, colorful kippot, and colorful head scarves for women, whether married or single. Judeo-Spanish also love bright colors, but often stick to earth tones—oranges and yellows. Men's kippot are always yellow or brown. One can tell Goth Jews—Faithers' chief intel gatherers in the tek-cities—from their dyed jet-black hair, no matter if they are dressing Conservative or Orthodox. Everyone greets Yonah with a "shalom" or "boker tov." He loves to be among his people—all God's tribes of Abraham, Moses, and Jacob.

It may be Sabbath for Protestants, Catholics, and Mormons, but Sunday is the traditional day for family food shopping at the market and the week's errands for Jews. Single people, couples, families, and pets—dogs and many more cats—are everywhere. Occasionally, he sees someone with a tek-rifle strapped over their shoulder—they even come with fashionable holo-skins these days to match one's clothing colors of the day. Like his own enclave in Florida, he imagines that every male and female above the age of thirteen is armed with some type of weapon or device.

He arrives at his destination within the enclave—the civilian government complexes. Here is where he will meet with the Jewish Continuum—the unified governing body of all the Orders of Judaism.

Yonah sits quietly on a bench in the hallway, his hat resting next to him. The walls are deep burgundy with a lamp about every three feet, and both the floor and ceiling are white marble. His piercing blue eyes stare straight ahead, his hands clasped in his lap. He is Yonah of the Orthodox Jewish Order, but he is also the famous Cowboy Rabbi.

A door opens at the far end of the hallway and a young man, almost a boy, runs to him. Dressed in black pants, a black vest over a white shirt—the tassels of a wool tallit katan dangling from beneath his vest—a black kippah on his head, and wearing glasses. He skids to a stop.

"Sorry, Mr. Cowboy Rabbi—"

Yonah stands, almost laughing. "I'm not wearing my double holsters, so I'm not the Cowboy Rabbi today. Please, call me Yonah. And shalom. What's your name, young man?"

The boy smiles. "Shalom, Mr. Yonah. I am Yosef."

"Nice to meet you, Mr. Yosef. Slow down and take a breath. The Messiah hasn't arrived yet."

The boy grins. "I'll take you there." He points down the hall. "They are waiting for you."

11:02 a.m.

Yonah is greeted with separate hugs by three men—Rabbi Oren, a senior elder in the Orthodox Jewish Order; Rabbi Henriques, senior rabbi in the Judeo-Spanish Order; and Mr. Tova, a senior leader of the Conservative Jewish Order. The men help themselves to food from the back table in the conference room, and the same boy enters with fresh pitchers of water and juice, placing them on the table before quietly leaving and closing the main door. The men take seats at the circular table in the center of the room and spend ten minutes or so making small talk.

"It's official?" Yonah asks.

"It is." Mr. Tova nods. "The Israeli Order will be no more by years' end, next month even."

Yonah shakes his head, incredulous. "I never thought I'd ever see it. It's been spoken of, but I never thought they would agree to it in the end with such intense feelings, even today. Not in my lifetime."

"People used to say that the Fall of Israel could never happen," Oren says, "because of God, because of the fact it was a gem in the Middle East. And like every corner of the Middle East, it would last until the end of time when even the sands of the desert would turn to dust. I always said that we were an oasis of the West stuck in the center of the Middle East and when the Fall of Western Europe happened it was only a matter of when, not if, it would come upon us too."

"We were separated from our Homeland once before. Eight hundred years. And we survived. Our enemies did not. It will be so again," Henriques says.

"We are all the Israeli Order now—the whole of the Jewish Continuum—in our hearts and souls, forever," Oren says.

"Yes, we are." Yonah nods. "Which Orders are getting the most of their members?"

"The Conservatives," Rabbi Oren answers, "and the Shamar Order. After that, it's the African Jewish Order and Mizrahi."

"Don't forget the thirty thousand joining the Judeo-Spanish Order," Rabbi Henriques adds with a smile. "And the Orthodox are taking in several thousand too."

"Mr. Yonah." Rabbi Oren's tone signals that the small talk is over. "Is your mind firm about presenting your proposal at this time?"

"There is never a best time in Faith World with the dangers we face."

"True, but there are better times. The Mormons excommunicated half their entire Order. The entire Continuum was pulled into what could only be called a mini-war, their own Mormon civil war. This fission bomb detonation business in the Russian Bloc. More troubling is the disappearance of the entire East Orthodox Christians and the Behemoth Project."

"Do we know anything more?" Yonah asks. "We have the best resources in the world and not one of our overseas assets can tell us what happened to them?"

"No. No one. They've disappeared and not even the Magi can tell us how or where. It's quite shocking, for many reasons, that half a million people can disappear."

"We'll never stop investigating," Mr. Tova says.

"Was it the Russians? The Caliphate?" Yonah asks.

"No one knows," Oren says.

"We're looking at all the superpowers, other nations, and even these Internationalists too," Mr. Tova says.

"None of us will stop looking for them. All the Orders are involved," Henriques says.

"With all of these issues, the upcoming full Continuum meeting already has a full agenda," Oren continues. "And the Catholics will not postpone their official selection ceremonies of Father Marcos as their new pope."

"It's going to be big," Rabbi Henriques says. "And a bigger security nightmare. One that they're not even accustomed to."

"The Continuum will be providing resources and so will the Magi," Mr. Tova adds.

"Good," Yonah says. "I do know it's not the best time by any means, but I believe my proposal is essential. I've put it off for a couple of years now, but this civil war of the Mormons, and the security threats to the Catholic Order's upcoming papal ceremonies, show that we're missing a needed tactical force. I wish to move forward as planned and see what the response of our Continuum is first."

Rabbi Oren nods. "Your proposal is both thorough and impressive. We read it several times."

Mr. Tova says as he stands, "Let's go see the *parents*."

Net-Comm Room
4:00 p.m., 21 October 2096

Yonah, Oren, Mr. Tova, and Henriques stand in a circular room with every inch of its walls, floor, and ceiling a shiny black surface—all holo-vid-screens, and a single light shines down on them from a floating, spherical photo-drone. They all face one way, standing nearly shoulder-to-shoulder.

In front of them, flickering light comes out of the blackness. A flashing green dot appears first, then dozens, hundreds of thousands, and millions, then billions, and more. The images of the attendees are all being beamed in from within Freespace—the corner of the Net not created, run, or monitored by governments.

The code becomes several people standing in front of them.

Two of the men are Mizrahi—Arab or Persian—from their bright traditional clothes and kippot, fuller beards and darker skin; and the third bearded man is dressed all in white attire with a white kippah. The woman is dressed business casual in purple, with shoulder-length, curly hair. All the holo-identities have a slight illumination to them.

One of the figures glows.

"I will commence this impromptu executive meeting of the Jewish Continuum. I, Tova Ben-Hurion of the Conservative Jewish Order. Hi, hon."

Mr. Tova smiles. "Hi, hon."

The glowing figure of Tova continues, "Rabbi Kanter of the Shamar Order, Rabbi Haza of the Arabic Jewish Order, Rabbi Nahai of the Persian Jewish Order; in live form at Masada, Rabbi Oren of the Orthodox Jewish Order, Rabbi Henriques of the Judeo-Spanish Order, my husband, Mr. Tova, also of the Conservative Jewish Order, and presenting is Yonah, also of the Orthodox Jewish Order. The Hasidim and African Orders are absent. Shalom, Yonah. Please begin."

"Thank you, Tova," Yonah begins. "And thank you, Round Table members. I am very cognizant of the upcoming full Continuum meeting regarding the serious events of the last few months. However, I believe this is precisely the time to move forward with my proposal.

"Each religious order has its own paramilitary force and we all readily and frequently work with the forces of every other Continuum member. But what we don't have is a paramilitary force for the full Continuum itself, made up of members from each Continuum member. The events of last August show us that such a force is long overdue. It would have a rotating leadership assignment structure, have both light-infantry and heavy-infantry capabilities, and most importantly, it could be deployed as needed by the Continuum. The Mormon's civil war should not have involved individual Continuum members—we put rules in place to prevent such things before we formed the Continuum and we were the Resistance. We were never supposed to get involved in the internal strife of another Order, let alone a civil war. The circumstances of the Mormon Order were unique, I acknowledge that, but we should have had coalition forces for the Continuum to use."

"Tell me, Yonah, how did you come up with this proposal?" the glowing figure of Rabbi Kanter asks. "Everyone knows you as the Cowboy Rabbi and one of the founders of the North American Underground Railroad. The proposal you submitted for review is very detailed."

"We have already done similar with the Underground Railroad. It is, at its core, a coalition of Jews, Protestants, and Catholics. Other Continuum members provide key support, including even the I-R-A. We can rescue slaves and relocate them from any point on the planet. My proposal is to replicate that coalition principle that we already utilize for the Underground Railroad and do the same for the Continuum."

"Do you have a name for this coalition?" Rabbi Nahai asks.

"You know I'm partial to cowboys. I was thinking of the Cowboy Coalition. Rangers seemed too bland to me."

"How many personnel would you propose starting with?" a glowing figure of Tova asks.

"A mere force of a thousand to begin with and expand as needed from there. With the Round Table's approval, I can get started at the full Continuum meeting."

"Do you have anything more to add?" Tova asks.

"No, my proposal alone suffices, but I can happily expand on any of the detail within it, if needed."

Tova's image says, "We'll discuss it among ourselves."

The holo-images of the attendees go out of phase for a few minutes. The men in the room wait quietly when the executive board returns to normal resolution.

"We approve the proposal," Tova says. "You can proceed as you see fit."

"Thank you," Yonah says. "Oren did mention that the Hasidim won't be able to participate."

"Nor will we," Rabbi Kanter's image interjects. "The Shamar Order has taken the lead on the new One Project. In some ways, it will be far more dangerous than your efforts forming this Cowboy Coalition."

Yonah is visibly displeased. "Truthfully, I believe the project is ill-advised."

"Perhaps. But it's either now or never," Kanter answers.

"Many of us would be happy with never."

"We understand, in the starkest way, the concerns of the Community. But we believe we have a vetting process that will satisfy all. And you might know him, but Mr. Elliott Finegold will be point on the preliminaries."

"Oh yes, Elliott. He's sharp. Good point person."

"The Hasidim will also be forming a new tactical force," Tova says to Yonah. "The Dog Corps."

"Hasidim hate dogs," Yonah says.

Some of the Jewish Continuum members laugh.

"Not anymore," Tova says. "These Hasidim will be training to fight with them—canine teams; one-man, one-dog tactical teams, both with robotic suit enhancements."

Yonah smiles. "Wonders never cease."

"And," Rabbi Oren adds, "teams of Hasidim and Orthodox women will be joining our new Continuum Medical Corps with the Amish and Mennonites. You didn't think you were the only one with the good ideas."

"Far from it."

"Gentlemen, thank you, and Yonah, good luck with your new endeavor," Tova says. "We all look forward to seeing this new Cowboy Coalition of yours. See you at the full Continuum Meeting."

The four men say goodbyes, echoed by the holo-attendees before their images vanish.

Kibbutzim, Idaho
8:02 a.m., 23 October 2096

In former Jewish Israel there were many kibbutzim—self-sustaining, collective communities that were traditionally centered on agriculture. After the Fall of Jewish Israel, millions of Jews re-settled all across America, mostly in the South and West. However, some of the more radical elements settled in the Northwest. Kibbutzim here are enclaves arranged in a network of compounds, each with a specific purpose: living, agriculture, livestock, water, defense, schools, vehicles, etcetera.

Elliott Finegold is far from militaristic—that honor would go to the Jewish skinheads known as the Wolf Pack, the lead tactical force for the Jewish Continuum. But he sometimes considers himself more dangerous—he's a lawyer. The forty-something counselor sits in his standard two-piece black office suit with a solid white shirt and black tie. He is a senior member of the Conservative Jewish Order, but keeps his offices here when not in the tek-cities arguing a case in the courts.

In his general sitting room is a white-haired man, one of the many judges that he has had the pleasure, and displeasure, of arguing before many years ago. Up until the 14th of June, 2080, sixteen years ago, the man was a Justice of the United States Supreme Court. That was the day the US Constitution was abolished, and soon after the American President abolished them—the entire US Supreme Court itself, in favor of a new Supreme Court under the new Rule of Law.

The two men sip their coffees, sitting across from each other with a small glass table between them.

Stein leans forward and declares, "I want in."

Elliott laughs. "Didn't you try to have me put in jail a few times?"

"More than a few times. Didn't you deserve it? Aren't all lawyers sons of bitches?"

"Some might say the same about judges."

"No, some would say worse of judges."

"In your courtroom I think I was doing what any zealous lawyer does."

"Meaning you were being as obnoxious and sneaky as possible. Well, I didn't put you in jail—though you deserved it. I still want in."

"What does that even mean? 'You want in.' You're a Pagan."

"So. You've got plenty of Pagans in your little outer Faither society."

"Did you just try to be subtly clever? Using the word Faither rather than the offensive term, Jew-Christian, in a complete sentence."

"Did it impress you?"

"Kinda." Elliott watches him. "Judge Stein, you were a sitting Justice of the Old Supreme Court under the T. Wilson administration."

"I was on the Court before he became President, and since there is no Old Supreme Court, just like there is no US Constitution anymore, I don't see how any of that past matters. I was thrown out on the sidewalk because I cast the only dissenting vote not to abolish the Constitution. I've been unemployable for life."

"Judge, I'm talking to you because I've known you a long time, but I'm not sure what you think I can do."

"Introduce me to people. I hear there is a whole pro-Faither atheist community in the Japan territories."

"Yes, but every one of them is vouched for by a Faither with unimpeachable credentials."

"You can vouch for me. You've known me for over twenty years now. You said so yourself."

"To vouch for someone is not a simple thing. It's actually a whole quasi-legal proceeding with impartial witnesses. It has to be certified. It says that if the one being vouched for goes afoul of Faither society, then both parties receive the same punishment. Vouching for someone is a very serious matter. My wife and kids will not be allowing me to vouch for anyone in this lifetime."

"You make it sound like it's not a common occurrence."

"It's not."

"I see."

"Why would you be pro-Faither? No wonder you can't get a job. Not very politically savvy, are you?"

"I'm always on the side of the underdog. That's just how I was made. The monkeys I evolved from were like that."

Elliott smiles. "Not every Faither will take to your brand of Pagan humor."

"Everyone likes humor."

"The Shogun."

"The Shogun?"

"They're the ones with the atheist community in Japan. And they're agnostics rather than full atheists."

"Same difference to me. So let them decide my fate. Let me be judged by other atheists whether I'm in or not."

"What are you going to tell them when they ask why you want to leave Tek World for our outer Faither societies, as you call it? Living with the underdogs is a somewhat weak argument, if I do say so myself, Your Honor."

Stein remains quiet for a moment and then says, "I'm old."

"That's it?"

"When you're old, you'll understand too. They won't leave me alone—the government. The bullying, the persecution. I can handle them—I've been doing so for six decades—but I want to live my end days in peace. That's not too much to ask. Surely you can understand such an argument. Wanting to be at peace and stop the fighting for once in your entire life, if even to see what it feels like."

"I understand, but do recognize that Faither communities are paranoid, xenophobic, and unforgiving."

"I'd expect that."

Elliott sets his coffee on the table. "I'll set it up then. I can do that, but these atheists you are so eager to petition before are…not nice people. They're ex-gangsters."

Stein waves his hand through the air. "Gangsters? That would describe most of the government thug agents that stood in my court. I can handle gangsters easily."

"Okay. I'll work on it and get back in touch with you."

"Good. I'll be waiting. Not that I have anything else to do with myself."

The men stand and Stein extends his hand, smiling. Elliott

shakes it with a smirk. Handshaking is a Faither custom; Pagans shunned it decades ago as an overtly 'religious' practice—though that is not its historical origin. Stein leaves through the open entrance and then out the main doors of the building.

Elliott walks out of the meeting room. His assistant sits at a desk writing on a tablet with her stylus pen. Dressed casually in tan, with her hair in a ponytail, she looks up at him angrily.

"Why must you try to help everyone?" she says with an annoyed tone. "Goth Lila told you to be careful. Once your name gets out there in the chatter-verse as a point-of-contact, all kinds of people will seek you out for every possible thing under the sun."

"Too late. I'm already permanently part of the chatter-verse."

"I don't know why you do it. Stick with our people. Here." She hands him his palm tablet.

"Who are 'our people'?" He reviews his messages.

"The Continuum is our people. That should keep you busy enough."

"Are you my sister or my mother, sis?"

"All sisters get double duty when it comes to their younger brothers."

He collapses the tablet to put in his jacket pocket.

"The Continuum will never allow him to join. He's a Pagan spy," she continues.

"You're so sure of that?"

"Yes, I am. His District handler must be overjoyed at his good fortune and thinks that because you've known him for so long that you'll be an easy dupe."

"I'm many things, but never an easy dupe. I'll be sending him to the Yakuza Fukkatsu."

"Oh." She smiles.

"Do you approve?"

"Oh yes, I do. They'll gut him and dump him in the ocean."

"Listen to my Jewish gangster sister talk. I think Stein is legit."

"He's a Pagan spy."

"They'll find out for sure."

"Dumped in the ocean. That's his only destination. Oh…are you speaking before the Continuum?"

"I don't think I should until after my preliminary meetings, but I will be at the general session."

She looks at him for a moment. "There seems to be a pattern with you."

"You don't approve again."

"Stein is nothing. Even if he were approved, he'd be living with Gnostics, away from us. This is our people, dear brother. We had three civil wars. No other Order has gone through so much internal turmoil as us. This route you and the others are taking…it could open up all those deep wounds. People will not live next to collaborators—no matter how far in the past, no matter how sincere their plea for forgiveness."

"These are our people and we should be together."

"When God flooded the Earth, I'm sure all those people outside the ark were sincere in their pleas for forgiveness to be allowed in. But God didn't tell Noah to open up the doors to them, did he?"

"So your words to the Exiles is what? Die?"

She doesn't hesitate. "Yes. And most feel as I do."

"Well, that I know. I'm only meeting with them. Nothing is decided."

"My brother has become a big softie. You thought as I do once."

"I listen to everyone—all points of view. I always have. Who's driving me there?"

"Tobias, and then you'll transfer to the Persians to take you the rest of the way. They'll be your security detail."

"Good. I'm off."

"And please be careful."

"I always am."

"Seriously. The Orthodox Christians vanish in Russia. The Russians exploding a fission bomb in peacetime against their own treaties, right in the vicinity of our own Continuum forces. The rumor is that they were deliberately targeting us."

"That is nonsense. The Russians did it as a show of force against the Americans, CHINs, and Caliphate."

Ignoring him, she says, "They say that their own president is literally transforming himself into some kind of monster and lives at the bottom of their presidential bunker and never comes out. That they send down chunks of animal meat to him."

Elliott shakes his head and laughs. "Where do these rumors come from?"

"I bet it's all true."

"They're wrong."

"Be careful."

"Yes, sis. I will."

"Always remember that Haman plots against us. Always. There are no coincidences in this world."

Midwest Wastelands (Trog-land), Florida
10:59 p.m., 23 October 2096

The black jet flies through the night only ten feet from the ground with an accompanying contingent of defense drones surrounding it.

Elliott reflects as he sits quietly in the center sitting compartment of his transport. Collaboration is a big sin in Faith

World. President T. Wilson—expected to sail into his fourth conservative term as American President with no end in sight—the man who sought to destroy all Faithers in America. Haman is the slur that Jews call him. The Christians, Galerius. The Mormons, Boggs. The historic Haman was the fifth-century BC noble of the Persian Empire who instigated a plot to kill all of the Jews of ancient Persia, but was foiled by Queen Esther. The Mizrahi feel as strongly against the Emperor Al-Siddiq of the Supreme Islamic Caliphate. The Shogun Christians feel the same against the Chinese-Indian Alliance (CHIN) President Ri Wen.

All around him sit his Persian security detail, armed, in robotic suits, and speaking loudly amongst themselves in their language. He's fluent in Persian too, but always pretends he can only speak Hebrew and English.

"We're arriving," one of the Persian bodyguards says to him in Hebrew. The man's cybernetic goggles make his pupils look like they are made of blue light.

Private High-Rise Apartment Complex, Florida Panhandle 7:50 p.m., 24 October 2096

He once met an Amish girl named Kristiana at a meeting who remarked to him that non-Anabaptist Faithers "speak so loud." They do. Elliott is the meeting's star attraction in the underground town hall room of this enclave housing complex of Exiled Jews. Their own building, their own security, and their own governing body. He views it as an odd set-up. He sits on an overly padded single-seater couch in the center, with one larger couch on one side with four leaders, and on the other an identical couch with an equal number of leaders. The audience of residents sits in folding chairs throughout the meeting room facing them, more arriving all the time. It reminds him of some kind of old-style television talk show. He was introduced to the less-than-enthused crowd. He feels their looks of disgust and contempt—he is the "enemy" to them, despite being invited. They hate everything about the Continuum and him—even despite the fact that no one else in the Continuum will talk to them. The leaders don't look or carry themselves as leaders should—they look to be in their pajamas. In fact, no one is dressed appropriately for a meeting as important as they claim it to be. One man sits in the front with nothing on but swim trunks and slippers. Half the crowd is half naked; the others are in sloppy casual clothes. Many stare at him like hawks. He fights his impulse to glare back at them and keeps his eyes roving. They are a surly, disrespectful, and angry bunch—far from 'shining examples' of Jewry. Elliott now wishes he were elsewhere.

As the questions come, Elliott realizes that he will be conversing with only the eight leaders assembled on the couches on either side of him.

"Aren't you registered with the government?" a woman asks.

"I'm registered with the government as a Jew so I can try legal cases before the government to defend Jews, Christians, and other Faithers. I'm proud of my efforts to keep the government away from us—physically and legally. Little pinpricks over time can do as much damage as a straight stab from a dagger. However, my registration is not the issue. Yours is. Most in the Continuum consider anyone who voluntarily allows themselves to be put in the Grid database to be untrustworthy."

"Everyone is in the Registry," a man challenges. "You're born and you're automatically in a database."

"Most of our citizens are not."

"That you know of. That you think. I bet they are. The government has every human in one database or another."

Elliott shakes his head. "Our people are not. We made sure of it."

The Registry is the Grid government's database of every American and non-citizen in the nation and is tied to everything: national identification file, national tax profile, national medical profile, and national census data. It is mandatory from birth, but Faithers and other off-Gridders do not register (and never have), which in itself is illegal.

"The first question they will ask—"

"Who's 'they'?" a man interrupts Elliott.

"I think you know who 'they' are. 'They' is our Jewish leadership. 'They' is the people who will not be amused by any attitude or subterfuge."

"What does that mean?" a woman asks. "We know what's said about us. They still think we're collaborators."

"Ma'am, you are collaborators." Elliott stares at her for a moment.

She averts her eyes as the constant chatter from the audience continues.

"That was many years ago," her husband says. "We've been punished. We've been exiled for almost three decades. When does it end? How many times do we have to apologize? We were kids back then—all of us were. The government had stormtroopers after us, spies everywhere, drones in the sky. We thought we were finished. We had Jews fighting each other in civil wars. We lost Jewish Israel. Then the Muslims took it over and then Muslims destroy Palestine Israel. We believed we had to work with the government to survive. To protect our families. To live. Why don't they understand that?"

"Sir, I'm not here to re-litigate the past. I am here to assess your current proposal. That's it."

"You're calling us liars," the woman says.

"I'm saying you are not being honest with the reasons you're telling me for wanting to rejoin us. And no, you haven't been exiled. It is far, far more serious than that. You've been excommunicated. To the Jewish Continuum, none of you exist."

"The Russians," another woman speaks up. "They're dropping bombs. We hear they're moving against all their religious citizens. Once again going after Jews. Our president is friends with theirs. We hear this Russian president is a demon, in truth, a demon monster. How long will it be before they start dropping bombs here too? The Russians were not the great champions they want us to believe in the last world war. The atheist Nazis invaded Poland to get the Jews. The atheist Communists invaded Poland to get the Jews. They'll start dropping bombs here too."

Elliott gives her a look. "What are you saying exactly? You all want to rejoin us, why? Because you feel they're going to drop bombs on us?"

"Yes," the woman answers. "Aren't you preparing for that?"

"Suicide. You called me here—this whole proposal is because you all want to commit suicide?"

"You make it sound so cheap. A people should be together as a people at the end, that's what it is," a man says.

Elliott takes a breath to calm himself as everyone watches him.

"We may have a lot of enclaves named Masada, but unlike the historical one, none of us is ever going to be killing ourselves in the face of enemies. Masada means 'a final stand' to us; we will retreat no further and if you confront us, we will throw you down the side of the mountain." He looks across the audience before looking back at the leaders. "No one is going to be dropping bombs on us. Your information is false. We also possess the means to protect ourselves from any attack, and the government knows it. That being said, I appreciate your sentiment, but we have no intentions of being obliterated anytime soon."

"That's what Jewish Israel said."

"We are not the government of Jewish Israel. Ladies and gentlemen, the hour is late and I have a long way to go."

"Wait." A woman stands. "You can't leave. We still want to rejoin. Can't we still do that?"

"But this is your home. The tek-cities are your home. Out in the wastelands is ours."

"We're not stupid, Mr. Elliott," another woman says. "We know you've built your own cities out there. We know you're thriving out there. You are thriving while we hide in the shadows here, shrinking and dying off. My own children want nothing to do with me. I did what I did for them. To be a mother for them. Raise them in safety. And they disown me and my husband because we won't renounce religion. We did it for nothing, all the sacrifice."

"I'm sorry to hear that, but it doesn't change the situation. You must find other options besides us."

"What about India or the Asian Consortium?" a man asks. "They speak English. Why not go there?"

"That's an option for you," Elliott answers.

"Sikhs and Hindus are there. They don't bother us," the man continues.

"Sikhs never. Hindus are split. But there are also Vampires, witches, and other anti-Faither groups there. And the region is surrounded by the Caliphate, the CHINs, and a new anti-Faither Russian Bloc."

"What about Canada?"

"They got more Muslims there than here."

"And then there's all those Star Trek people—Vulcans and the rest," a woman says with disgust.

"They don't bother us," Elliott says.

"Where are all those Jedi idiots?"

"The West Coast," an old man answers.

"Where do the Mormons hide?" another leader asks Elliott. "You never see them, but we know they have a lot of people."

"I won't be answering that question—ever. So is this about rejoining the Jewish community or finding out where everyone is hiding, to use your completely erroneous term?"

"We're hiding and so are you. You just want to pretend you're not. We're at least honest about it."

Elliott looks at him. "We don't hide." He realizes immediately that he has lost his calm, cool composure again. They've gotten under his skin, he says to himself. A complete breach of his lawyerly demeanor. The man is smiling in triumph, realizing what he has accomplished.

"Seems like you really don't like us," he says.

"I could have told you that beforehand and saved myself a trip. You are asking the wrong questions. You have the wrong attitude. You're not even dressed appropriately for a meeting as important as you claim it to be. The others won't meet with you. So if you don't like me, then that's too bad. I'm all you got. In legal terms there's what's called a grace period. The two parties go to their own corners and let some distance and time pass. You and I need a grace period. You need to decide if you're really serious about moving forward, because it will not be easy, and ultimately, and very likely, you will be denied. I also need to decide if I want to move forward with you. Because should a miracle happen and you jokers do get in, it will be my name associated with you forever. I need to think more about that. Because I'm not convinced you will behave yourselves."

"Behave ourselves. What does that mean? Will your enclaves

micromanage how we behave too?"

"If I have to explain it to you, then we should end this before we get started. You all obviously have no shred of individual or group dignity that you care about, but I have a reputation that I have established over three decades that I do actually care a lot about."

"Mr. Attorney?" a black-haired woman calls out from in the audience.

The leaders are visibly irritated by the breach of protocol.

"Elliott, please, ma'am."

"I prefer to call you Mr. Attorney. In the law, Mr. Attorney, if I shoot at you and the pulse blast misses, hits right next to your head, I am not charged with murder, even if that was the intent. Correct? I am charged with what did happen, not with what could have happened. Is not your Continuum judging us on what could have happened rather than what did?"

"The Resister-Registrant wars were back in the '70s and '80s. We're in the late '90s now, almost to the next century. It's over and this childish feud should be over too," a male leader says.

"Since a lot of people lost loved ones in that conflict, I would strongly advise you never to use the phrase 'childish feud' in front of them," Elliott says.

"I'm sorry. You know what I mean."

"We don't have to solve everything tonight. I committed to come and listen with no promises, and I did. I know what the threshold is and you haven't met it. But you all knew that without me having to say it."

"It smells of vindictiveness," the black-haired woman says.

"Really? It seems a bit of revisionist history is taking root, because I remember many in this very room—and yes, I do remember some of you—saying it would be a cold day in

Gehenna—Hell, for those of you not up on your Jewish terms—when you'd ever want to rejoin the Community."

The black-haired woman looks away.

"There's plenty of vindictiveness to go around, but it didn't originate from our side. I think I should go."

"Haven't excommunications been overturned before?" a man asks.

Elliott stops and looks at him. "I'm sorry, but it is rare."

A young woman stands from her chair and walks to him. Elliott realizes that she is actually a girl, dressed in black with a blue baseball cap on a bald head.

"Bald head? What's that for, young lady?"

She smiles. "You definitely aren't any kind of Jew from here. No one says 'lady' or 'gentleman,' 'ma'am,' or 'sir' in this place. Only a real Faither has manners like that." She looks at the gathering. "Aren't they all so pathetic?" she says. "The only good thing about living in Tek World is that you can divorce your parents. Here the kids are absolutely smarter than the parents. Were you there?"

"There where?" Elliott asks.

"The Fall of Jewish Israel."

Elliott at first doesn't know how he should react. After a long pause, he answers. "I was."

The girl moves closer. "You lived there?"

"No, I joined the emergency IDF. Flew from America on some of the first planes out. I was one of thousands of American Jews to get out before the travel ban."

"What stands out? What remains with you most from when you were there?"

Elliott reflects and answers without looking at her. "The screams." He looks at her.

The girl's eyes widen. "People screaming?"

"The cats." He pauses again. "There were many plans to evacuate people, but no one thought of the cats. They were everywhere—crying. They sounded like…screaming children. I often wondered if that's how it was back in the Holocaust. They said there was no screaming. It all happened so fast, but I always wondered. There were so many of them, cats left abandoned. I had more nightmares of those screams than of dead people. Will never happen again, though. Every rescue plan always accounts for pets and animals—every one. That's why there are so many cats in Jewish enclaves today. It's like penance. Bet the Pagans don't even know that's where all the abandoned cats go. We take them."

Elliott realizes that not only is the girl transfixed to what he's saying, but so is everyone in the auditorium.

"I wanted to tell you," the girl says, "that if you decide not to take them, that we kids want a separate hearing. You'll be impressed with us, I promise. I want to join the Jewish Wolf Pack." She smiles. "Shoshana, the Iron Rose, is my idol. I want to be just like her. And there are many of us—girls and boys. Will you promise to let the kids have a separate hearing?"

"How old are you?"

"Fifteen. Age of reason."

"Yes, I think you deserve your own hearing."

She smiles again. "Well, nice to meet you, Mr. Elliott. I can't stay any longer in the same auditorium with them or I'll throw up."

Elliott holds back a smile.

"Those are my bio-parents." She gestures with her head to the very male and female leader closest to him on the couch.

Her parents are both completely unaffected by her insults. "You said excommunication reversals are rare, but it is possible?" the man asks Elliott. "I mean, if we were able to trade or *buy* our way back into the Community."

Elliott's eyes narrow. "And how would you do that?"

"Offer something the Continuum would really want in exchange."

"Such as?"

"Information."

"What information?"

"Information that would be of immense value to the Continuum."

"Sir, I don't like games."

"It's not a game. It's not a game to anyone in this room. We know you don't like us. We know the Continuum doesn't want us and is more than content with watching us die in exile. We know, Mr. Elliott. We know how we're regarded, and, honestly, the feelings have always been mutual. You have called us collaborators. We have called you religious zealots. But that's past. It's over. We lost. You won. I'm over it. We all are."

"Just forgive and forget, is it? The Continuum does not believe in transformative reconciliation. You do something against us and you will never be in a position to do it again. We forgive—if we don't kill you—but we never forget."

"I think you will."

Elliott frowns, fighting his impulse to walk out of the auditorium.

"We will give you information to hand over to the Continuum that will prove to all of you that the reason our anti-Jew-Christian"—he corrects himself seeing Elliott's reaction—"our anti-Faither government has left you alone for all this time, along with all the Trog anarchists and Outland separatists, is because the government hasn't left you alone. All of you in your own isolated, self-segregated ghettos wrapped up for them with a big red bow."

"Enclaves are not ghettos," Elliott snaps back. "And one could say the same about them in their tek-cities."

The man laughs. "You didn't think all the government had was their Rabbi Susan, Bishop Joe, and Master Pastor collaborators-in-chief?" his wife asks.

"Spoken by someone who would know," Elliott snaps again.

She glares at him.

"It's strangely biblical. You fatten the cow to the right size before you kill it," the husband adds.

Washington Hilton Hotel Ballroom, Washington, DC
6:30 p.m., 4 June 2089 (Seven Years Earlier)

President Wilson has not been seen in public for many months. The event is a special fundraiser of his major donors in the District. It is a tuxedo affair for the men and little black dress affair for the women.

Mrs. Lucifer is rolled into the banquet room by her cyborg husband. She may be in a wheelchair, but she is stunningly dressed.

"Hades, my God, you look amazing. And you just came out of a coma. How do you do it?" one of the women says—everyone is noticing her.

She smiles and says, "Don't you know ninety is the new fifty?"

President Wilson gives a good speech. He smiles and waves as the attendees applaud.

The Supreme Senate has enacted a law banning any presidential action against any Jew-Christian ghetto without the explicit approval from a majority of the nation's governors. They would only allow action against a Jew-Christian enclave in the nation if the administration could prove that the enclave was behind a specific act of terrorism. Congress supported the law.

The National Police Chiefs Association has also banned the use of stormtroopers for any federal action not approved by the Supreme Senate. The president of the NPCA said, "I have enough funerals to attend to carry me well into the next decade."

The entire intelligence community had been consumed with locating the missing American jets. The Northern Confederacy floated the idea of intervening on behalf of the White House and opened a dialogue with the Jew-Christians. Later, the jets were "found"—delivered, disassembled, to the Asian Consortium.

Wilson used the return of the jets to overshadow his defeats to the Supreme Senate and the NPCA—and it has worked.

"Mr. President. It looks like we both seem to have come back from the dead," Mrs. Lucifer says, smiling. The president has moved from the stage to meet the attending donors at the event.

"Thank you, Mrs. Lucifer. Yes, we are both survivors."

"Yes, we are."

He continues to mingle in the crowd with his Secret Service detail close. They move him from the VIP section of the banquet, with its one hundred major donors, to the general area, where thousands of people wait behind a partition—smiling, cheering, and reaching out their hands to greet him. He immediately walks to them. Such events where a celebrity of some sort meets a crowd are the only times Pagans do shake hands. Wilson does so with a large smile on his face. He has managed to survive another crisis.

The man in the red fedora extends his hand to the president. The man is smiling and unthreatening, but instead of shaking the president's hand, he reaches in and pokes him in the center of his chest with his index finger.

"The finger of God," he says and starts to walk backwards.

President Wilson is unnerved and his Secret Service detail is already calling in on their ear-sets to apprehend the man. The man seems to be enveloped by the crowd. Plainclothes Secret Servicemen rush into the crowd from three different sides. The man ducks down into the mass of people. They can't see him. The three Secret Servicemen reach the spot and all there is, lying on the ground, is the red fedora. The man is gone.

The lead Secret Service agent takes no chances. They surround the president and whisk him out a side door to the secure parking lot and into the presidential limousine. Agents swarm into the banquet hall to detain the entire body of attendees.

Mrs. Lucifer starts to laugh. "Let's get out of here, husband. We've done our evil deed. Our little temporary alliance with the Jew-Christians is over. Let's disappear into the night before our good and dear friend, the president, sends a kill team after us too, like he did to our son."

Toronto, Canada
2:12 p.m., 1 October 2096

Ever-flashing, ever-changing digital billboards adorn the top of every commercial building in the tek-city—advertising music, movies, clothes, the latest devices, latest cars, restaurants, vacation trips, virtual reality dens, drug parlors, or massage services. These advids are either rapid stop-motion, live-def static photos, or full-fledged vids. The colors are as bold and vibrant as the sounds are loud and frenetic. Both rapidly pulsate to create an atmosphere that completely engulfs the sight and hearing of anyone within range. Surveillance drones zip around more than a hundred feet in the air or hover in mid-air.

A lone man walks a few steps up the sidewalk and stops again to engage in people watching. The streets are packed and brimming with life, energy, and excitement. There is nothing like the hustle and bustle of a tek-city, both the automation and the people. The obsolete adjective is technological and the obsolete noun is technology, but no one under the age of eighty uses those words anymore—the word is *tek*. It isn't just slang that, after a few decades of common use, has replaced its original reference; it's an attitude.

Along with many others, the balding man comes out of the metro exit for the fast-track (train) onto the street. People are in traditional business office suits or casual attire, in a variety of colors from simple blacks and whites to earth tones to natural rainbow colors to synthetic, techno colors, or even the so-called futuristic shiny silver everything. Everyone is carrying or wearing their device of choice—e-pads, tablets, ear-set, interfaced glasses, etc.

Dressed in a casual white office suit, he walks up the three flights of stairs to his apartment home as he does daily.

"Morning, Mr. Gee." His next-door neighbor pops out of her front door as he passes. The brunette in a blue halter top dress playfully smiles with a glass of shimmering yellow alcohol in her hand.

"Morning, Ms. Cubex."

"I'm having a house party today. Stop by if you have the time."

"I may do that."

He continues down the very wide hallway to his apartment door and it automatically opens at his approach. She watches him disappear inside before taking another sip from her glass.

"Oh, I forgot to tell him what time," she says to herself.

She ducks back into her apartment to place her glass on a corner table and runs barefoot to his place. The door is only half closed, which surprises her. All interior shades are down so there is very little light inside.

"Mr. Gee?"

She moves inside slowly and sees a fallen body behind the door on the floor with the legs sticking out. Someone else is moving inside. She screams and runs back out.

A nearby police drone hears the scream and flies to the scene with sirens beeping.

Vatican Games

**Jungle Compound, Brazil
9:03 a.m., 1 October 2096**

Deafening sirens shriek from outside of the fortified compound—a two-story, gray pyramid design. The secluded property is enclosed by a ten-foot, 'sticky' razor-wire wall with an arch over the metal gate. Gun-toting men run out of the building and jump into SUVs, Jeeps and trucks parked in a semi-circle around the building. Three more men burst out from the doors.

"Blow it," the center man commands, wearing a neon silver office suit with an open white shirt.

The man on his left pushes a button on a hand-held device and the entire compound erupts in flames. Both of his men are in rugged, casual clothes.

"What's happening, boss?" the other man asks.

"Unidentified jets are headed to us. The Invisible Fighters. It must be them. They're hitting all our facilities."

"Which ones?"

"All!"

"All?"

"All! Everything! We're the only ones left."

"They would need an army on the ground and air to hit all of us at the same time. The government would never allow that."

"The government is a joke. We should know because we made them that way. We need to be away from here."

"We shouldn't have blown the bunker. We could have stayed there and dug in."

"No. We had the bunkers, but nothing was stocked. I'm not getting buried in a bunker with no food and water. We're safer outside where we can see. We have the drones in the air watching all the roads and they'll shoot anything on the ground or air that approaches. No one could get in here unless they run all the way through the jungles and up to us." The boss man talks into his wrist. "What's taking so long?"

"They're loaded," a voice says from the device on the leader's right wrist.

He answers into his wrist-comm. "Get in the air!"

"Boss, are we sure?" his man asks. "Every single girl we got is on those transports. That's all our money in the world on those three transports. A lot of money."

"The Invisible Fighters would never shoot them out of the air. They're safer than us. Let's—"

"Are those two of our girls?" The other man points. They all take notice.

Two women are already through the gates, running at breakneck speed to them in army green, two-piece bikinis and jungle boots.

"Who are you two?" the leader yells. The other two men are grinning.

Before he can say another word, the first twin throws two

daggers at them. It flies from her hand—already laser-locked—at the men. It slices through the bodies of two of the men, who immediately collapse to the ground. The shocked leader runs, but is stabbed in the head with a laser dagger by the other twin. He falls to the ground dead.

The cartel henchmen waiting in the vehicles look at each other before reacting. Some vehicles drive off while other men jump out to shoot at the women with machine guns and rifles. Mortar rounds begin to fall; vehicles are hit, and explode. Bodies are thrown everywhere.

The twins ignore the carnage of the entire convoy of the slave smugglers being destroyed and watch the compound on fire. Humanoid drones fly over them, descend to the ground, and immediately run into the blaze shooting white-water from their hand sockets to put out the fire.

Civilian soldiers dressed in camo-green fatigues pour through the gate and fan out throughout the grounds. A squad runs to them. One is a female soldier who hands the twins their fatigues. The women quickly put them on.

"When the fire is out, we want every inch scanned by bloodhound-teks," says one twin.

"Yes, ma'am," answers one of the soldiers.

"If there is any surviving data in there, we want it. This is their data center. These criminals don't like their data on the Net."

"Destroying computer consoles and data banks is easy, ma'am. Erasing the data is not," says one soldier.

More civilian soldiers run to them.

"Ma'am, we missed the transports. They're already gone."

"How far out?" asks the other twin.

"A minute out—max."

"We'll intercept. Get the fire-bots out and the bloodhound teks in and let's get in the air. "

The lead jet flies low, just above the jungle canopy, with several others following. Inside the Twins sit behind the dual pilots, watching the monitors.

"Have the Medical Corps standing by," one Twin says to the pilots.

"Contacting them now, ma'am," the comm-pilot answers.

In the cargo area behind the Twins, the crew of forty sit in floor pods, each able to swivel three hundred and sixty degrees.

"Can I ask you a question, ma'am?"

The Twins take their eyes from the monitor to swivel in their own chairs to look back at the female soldier.

"Which one?" one Twin asks.

The soldier smiles. "Both," she answers. "We rarely have the opportunity to talk to the command staff."

"There's no command staff in the Underground Railroad. We have conductors, engineers, caretakers, shepherds, and telegraphers, but all of us are equals. We're here to rescue the packages and kill slavers so they can make no more slaves."

"How did you both get involved? I mean…nuns as commanders."

"There's no contradiction in God's eyes," one Twin answers. "Clergy and laity are both commanded to fight evil. We are all the New Catholic Order. No one is above you. We're all sinners. We're equal."

"Yes, Sister. I mean…ma'am."

"Our family," the other Twin answers. "Our father and brothers brought us to it."

"Oh, they helped rescue slaves too?"

"No." The Twin shakes her head. "They were slavers."

The soldier is surprised by her answer.

"They were among the worst in Bolivia. Dear papa and our five brothers. Papa raised us to be little angels. That's how they kept us quiet for so long. They told us that these girls weren't family. We were special and not to worry about what happened to these girls."

"We started asking questions. 'Androids can never replace human flesh,' Papa would say to us. 'It's simply business,' he would say. It was Papa who sent us to church. He was a godless bastard but thought church people would keep us passive."

"Their plan backfired," the other Twin said. "Sending us to religious school made us more anti-slavery, not less. They thought we would come out as meek little flowers. Unfortunately for them, we became just the opposite."

"It gave us God," the other Twin continues. "We knew what good and evil was. But it gave us the reasoning and the arguments for action. That is what we were missing and that's what we got."

The soldier hesitates to ask. "What happened to them?"

"Jungle people are not like rural or city people. We're very similar to desert people. In those cultures, one takes care of your own problems. No one calls the police or government authorities. The people handle their own affairs, even for a loved one who has strayed onto the evil path. They ran the largest slaver operation in three countries. And when my sister and I turned eighteen, with only a dagger each—family heirlooms going back a century—well, when we turned nineteen, there were no more slaver operations in Bolivia."

"Never any doubts? Hesitations?"

The Twins smile. "Doubts?" one asks. "That's city sentimentality. But we know what you mean—vigilantism, street justice, or, in our case, our own holy war. No, these were not crimes according to us. These are crimes according to everyone. We use the secular law to judge these as crimes. But in the Spanish

Americas where so much of the corrupt government is controlled by cartels and their puppets, crimes are ignored, police too afraid to arrest, courts too afraid to prosecute, juries too afraid to convict, judges too afraid to sentence and lock up. Who then is to protect the innocent? There are no self-doubts and self-recriminations here. These are God's innocent children and they must be protected."

Organization of the Spanish Americas Headquarters, São Paulo, Brazil
11:12 a.m., 1 October 2096

The tek-city metropolises of the Spanish Americas are surrounded by jungles. Their construction reflects that global uniqueness—green-tinted metallic structures and natural tree and plant life incorporated into buildings, including bird habitats, and many open, man-made rivers and brooks.

The United Nations is long gone. It was blamed for the Fall of Western Europe with the Muslim world forming the Supreme Islamic Caliphate right out of its body in 2065. Though none of the world's three superpowers are members—America, the Caliphate, and the Chinese-Indian Alliance—the Organization of the Spanish Americas proudly patterns itself after the former intergovernmental body and replaced the Old Organization of American States, which the region viewed as an American puppet organization.

The OSA headquarters is in the nation's largest tek-city housed in a majestic white building with giant flags of every Spanish American nation, from Mexico to Central America to South America, encircling the structure in three separate ring formations. São Paulo is a tale of two cities, like most of the Spanish Americas, with the wealthy traveling in their spacious, faux hover-limos and personal heli-jets, and the poor with their pedi-bikes, moto-bikes, franken-cars (pieced together from old and new car parts), and on public transportation.

A group of men hastily move past people in the large, stately hallway to the elevators.

"We'll catch them before they can get to the Assembly Hall," the Assistant Secretary General says.

"What's the fear?" one of the diplomats asks.

"We believe they plan to use the general assembly as a forum for an illegal protest today. The Secretary General feels they may even try to embarrass the OAS and the presidents of many Spanish American countries with their propaganda."

"Why can't we just bar this Fontana from even entering?"

"She's the daughter of an OAS Emeritus member. Politically we can't do that. Barring her would only help her cause."

"What is it that these women want? The Spanish Americas has done more to stop the sex slave trade than the United States, CHINs, Caliphate, and Russian Bloc combined."

Outside OSA Headquarters, São Paulo, Brazil
10:02 a.m., 1 October 2096

Every historic landmark and government center in Brazil has its own public transportation hub with at least one dedicated stop. Ms. Fontana arrives with her group of a dozen women by way of the fast-track—the nation's monorail transportation system. The women are dressed stylishly, but conservatively—collectively in all the bright colors of the rainbow. One woman stands out—Sister Serena. The only indication that she is a Catholic nun in her modern knee-high, black dress and white flats is her white scapular and rear black head covering. She also has a black patch over her left eye. They exit, along with locals, employees, tourists, and delegates, all in conversation.

"I'm wondering if you're the same Persia I've heard of," Serena asks one of the women, dressed in white with a multi-colored neck scarf, and her curly hair down past her shoulders.

"I'll save you the suspense. I am," the woman answers. "We've never met, but we have all the same mutual acquaintances."

"What brings you along to our band of merry women? You're based in the US and Caliphate territory, aren't you? I can't imagine you have any peoples in the Spanish Americas."

"True, and yes, I am, but one can never learn too much. We want to help and learn as much as we can. You've been at the slave rescue business longer than us."

"The Protestants have been at it for at least two decades before us Catholics. The Jews started around the same time as the Protestants. The American Separatist movement made a lot of groups steadfast allies. The Spanish Americas had some unique issues we had to deal with." Serena looks at the looming building. "And we're about to enter one of those centers of chaos."

The women chuckle.

"We all must behave," Fontana scolds. "They will purposely try to stir us up so they have an excuse to remove us from the assembly hall and keep us from speaking. Be calm and even-toned at all times, even if one of them makes you so angry you want to punch him in the face."

"I'm a nun," Serena says, "and they know me as a member of the Underground Railroad, but I started my work life as a teacher. Everyone thinks I was military or some women's mixed-martial arts fighter beforehand. But it was school books before machine guns. I got into this because they snatched a couple of my students. And I was going to get them back to their families. Patience is part of my DNA. Try managing a schoolroom full of possessed little Spanish boys. You survive that and there is no trial on the planet you can't get through. Even a room full of stupid diplomats."

The women have to walk the quarter mile to the entrance. There are no people-mover walkways or other transportation means by design. Security takes another half hour—walking past watchful male and female guards through an array of scanning arches and See-Thru tek-walls to the elevators. Fontana and her party exit the elevators on the lower main level and are immediately greeted by a waiting Assistant Secretary General, along with two aides and about a dozen diplomats. The man is dressed like they all are: dark shiny office suits, ties, and shoes.

"Ah, Ms. Fontana, I'm glad we caught you before you and your party were seated."

"Good afternoon, Mr. Assistant Secretary General. Is there a problem?"

The man is friendly and smiling, but his two aides are stone-faced.

"We appreciate that you wished to have your guest speak in your place, but the Secretary General cannot get the approval of the General Assembly."

The group of male delegates stand behind the Assistant Secretary General as if they are his bodyguards.

"Why not? I am a delegate."

"And as such, you must get the votes of the majority to allow any guest speaker to address the Assembly. You know why this rule is in the by-laws."

"By-laws? This was all arranged. That's why we are here. I got approval months ago. If I hadn't, we wouldn't be here today."

The man ignores her anger. "Without following these rules, we'd have every member nation inviting unacceptable, controversial, offensive speakers and, in no time at all, we would have no OSA at all. The Assembly cannot allow any guest speakers that are not citizens of the Spanish Americas."

"Excuse me? Why? That is illegal? We have never had such a rule before. We've had foreign guests and speakers before."

Serena steps forward. "Sir, I was born in Venezuela. Has my country been expelled by the OSA? If so, then it will be news to my nation."

"But you are not a sanctioned representative of that country."

"Why do I need Venezuela's permission to speak before the OSA about the crisis of sex-slavery and women in the Spanish Americas?"

"You must be sanctioned by a member country. However, if Mexico sanctions you…"

Serena smiles. "You would like me to do that, wouldn't you? So you could try to sanction Mexico. I know your member states are trying to formally get the Underground Railroad classified as a terrorist organization. I am here as a private citizen and women's advocate."

"It is," a male delegate says.

"What is?" Ms. Fontana asks.

"The Underground Railroad is a terrorist group. I may support most of its activities, but it is still a terrorist group."

"It is certainly not," Fontana snaps at him.

"There wouldn't be an Underground Railroad if any of your governments did their part in the slave wars." Serena adds.

"I take great offense to that," the Assistant Secretary General says. "Brazil leads the way in South America against global slavery."

"Easy to do when no one else is doing anything," she answers back. "Especially a country with so many consumers of illegal sex-slaves."

"That is a slanderous lie and I demand you to retract it!" a diplomat yells.

"Please," the Assistant says to them. "I would point out that no other country in the Spanish Americas does more to root out sex slave traffickers than Brazil. Our military makes attacks and arrests daily."

"The military could wipe it out in a day if it went after the consumers too," another woman angrily says.

The Assistant ignores her and looks at Fontana. "Ms. Fontana, I'm sorry, but I did try."

"I am not even worthy enough for the Secretary General to speak to me directly like a human being."

"You know it's political. He can't be seen with you. It is not personal and you should not take it personally."

"Will any of my party be allowed to address the general assembly?"

"No, Ms. Fontana. We can't allow any."

"What about the atheist women?" Fontana asks.

"None. We allow one, we have to allow all."

"This is an outrage!"

"Take your religious zealots away from here," another man says.

"Religious zealots?" Serena asks. "Are you saying that only religious people care about Spanish Americas' children being snatched into slavery? Is that what you're saying, Mr. Atheist?"

"No, I am not saying that…"

"Or is this a chauvinistic sexist play on your part? They snatch boys and men too, you know. This is the post-pan-sexual world after all. Come to think of it, you have a very plump butt, sir. You'd look nice in some high heels."

The man turns a bright red and a few of his colleagues have to stifle laughs. The man turns and storms off.

"I demand you allow my guest to be heard," Fontana yells at

the men.

"Sister Serena," the Assistant Secretary speaks directly to her. "The OSA is against all forms of slavery—labor or sex. That is fact. We will not allow propaganda on the floor of the Assembly to the contrary, and we cannot allow those with questionable credentials to speak before this body."

"Not even international organizations representing the very people of the Spanish Americas?" Fontana asks.

"The Underground Railroad organization, no matter its cause, operates outside of any formal government and outside of international law. It conducts paramilitary operations, not formally sanctioned by any government."

"Rescuing slaves is a dirty business, sir, because you're dealing with dirty people," Serena says.

"Have these men-killers escorted out of the general assembly room. Now! Leave now!" a newly-arrived male delegate yells.

The crowd of men behind the Assistant Secretary grows.

"I may not be here as a formal representative of the Mexican government, but I am a formal representative of the Bishop of New Lerdo, Durango, Mexico and of the New Catholic Order. We are a civilian religious organization separate from the formal government of Mexico…until the next Mexican election."

"What do you mean by that?" the Assistant Secretary asks. "Theocracies are illegal everywhere in the Spanish Americas."

"Too bad narco-governments and their state buffoons are not," Fontana interjects and the men scoff.

"I agree with America and the CHINs on that," the diplomat adds, "not much else, but I agree with religious exclusion for public office. Religious people should not be allowed to hold office. But that is for our courts to decide."

Serena continues, with the men closely paying attention to her.

"After the elections, Mexico might see fit to introduce resolutions that any pro-slaver nation—those that legally support the practice and those that participate in the practice—be immediately expelled from the OSA and severe economic sanctions be placed on them."

The men are aghast.

"Such a resolution would never pass the general body," the Assistant Secretary says confidently.

"And if the OSA would not see fit to support such a resolution, then we would call for the complete dissolution of the entire OSA and have it join all the other useless world bodies of the past, such as the League of Nations and the United Nations that either ignored rising evil or were active collaborators. Will I be allowed to speak?"

Assistant Secretary glares at Serena. "No."

"Interesting," Serena says to Fontana. "They give women leadership roles in the anti-slave wars while the men participate on the back end."

"I don't have to stand here and listen to slanders of a religious fanatic."

"Sister Cyclops. Do you know that name?" another man in a white suit speaks up for the first time.

"Who might you be?"

"Why?" the man asks.

"I always like to know the names of the people I know I'll be having problems with in the future."

"I am Mr. Khan, Sister Cyclops," he says.

She walks through the men to him. "Mr. Khan, is it? What is it that you said about the Portuguese language? I heard your talk at one of your surrogate campaign speeches on the road during your president's campaign."

He smiles. "You know me. I said, it is the true language of the gods. Language is why America was so powerful in the past. Their language became the international language—or I should say the Old British, because America is just an off-shoot of them, as Ancient Rome was an off-shoot of Ancient Greece. They assimilated their empire and renamed everything, but it was the same, just bigger. People speak your language; they become your people without even realizing it."

"What is your actual occupation, Mr. Khan?"

"I'm a linguist by profession, but these days I serve my president in communications."

"A language fascist. Interesting. And if you had your way, you'd erase all that lowly Spanish from the mouths of the Spanish Americas."

"That's not what I said or even implied, nor have I ever said or implied that. To want your own language to be the international language is not fascism."

"I bet you wish we went back to the old term for the Spanish Americas—Latin America, was it? Whatever that was."

"Every person in the world prefers to have their own group supreme above all others. You imaginary god believers are no different. It's amusing that one brainwashed by religious dogma would even use the word fascist."

"Actually, we are different, Mr. Khan. We want to be left alone to live, work, raise our families, worship in peace, and that's it. If you Darwinians and Muslims didn't mess with us, I'd be some obscure person in the outbacks of Venezuela, selling trinkets to tourists along the beach in bright red dresses during the week and worshiping, singing, and dancing in church on Sundays. For every action there is an equal and opposite reaction. I am who I am today because of your people, Mr. Khan." She smiles. "Look at that, Mr. Khan. You're like a god. You created something—the new; us. Now you're upset what you created is better and smarter than you. If you had stopped interfering with the people of the Hebrew Bible, you would already be at the top of the food chain. Ironic, isn't it?"

Khan is not amused by her. She can see the contempt in his eyes.

"Innocent people being kidnapped and forced into sex slavery and labor slavery. Modern abolitionists not being allowed to speak before government bodies about it. It's my fellow religious dogmatic cultists rescuing these women and boys. What are your godless cultists doing about it? Should we ask these victims and their families which cult they prefer? You're a presidential staffer. Commission a national poll and let's find out."

Mr. Khan stays quiet.

Ms. Fontana looks at the Assistant Secretary again. "That's exactly why I invited my guests. Because the people know exactly what the issues are, but you elites never do. This isn't about pride or your honor. This is about innocent women. These are Brazilian women…Spanish American women. Were you not born of a woman, or are we mistaken?"

"Don't waste your breath," Serena says to her and looks at the man in white again. "No, Mr. Khan, I can see the future. The eye that is covered by my patch sees the future. It sees the darkness in others. It sees you as it's seen so many others before you." She turns away from him and focuses on one of the other women of Fontana's group—Persia. She hugs her and says, "I'm so sorry."

Persia doesn't know what she means. Serena walks past the men into the general assembly auditorium as they watch her.

The Assistant Secretary looks back at Fontana. "What is she doing? None of them are allowed to speak."

He follows with the men around him. Fontana and her group

trail in after them. Serena is talking to a little boy in one of the rear seats a few yards away. Khan tries to hide his surprise, but says nothing as the group stops in place.

The interior of the general assembly auditorium is massive, open, and concave in structure, with the top of the ceiling twenty feet up. At the head of the auditorium, behind the rows of member nation seats, are giant flags on translucent poles, three rows, of each of the Spanish American nations.

Khan says to himself, *"Why is she talking to my son?"*

"What's that under your chair, young man?" Serena asks.

The boy hesitates in answering. "I have to pretend it's not here. I'll get in trouble."

"Is that a real hover-board? The one you can do all those tricks with?"

"Yeah."

"How far can it hover?"

"One and a half meters off the ground, but it can shoot you up."

"Very good."

"What are you supposed to be?"

"Me? I'm a nun of the Catholic Order."

"Oh, a church lady. My parents say church people are stupid."

"That isn't a very nice thing to say, young man, to people who you don't even know. You should be nice to everyone, except for those doing bad or evil things to others. What if I was to make such assumptions about you? We wouldn't be having this friendly conversation."

"What does the Catholic Order do anyway?"

Sister Serena puts her hands on her hips. "Do you want to talk religion or hover-boards?"

The boy starts laughing. "You know what I'm going to say."

"So do we have a deal or what?"

"Deal? What deal?"

She leans down and whispers to talk to the boy.

The men watch but they are too far away to hear. The Assistant Secretary looks back at Fontana. "I said what I said, so I will continue with my duties. Please keep your party in observance of the assembly guest rules or they will be escorted out by security."

"Why are you doing this?" Fontana asks. "These are our girls. Our boys. Our children. Crimes against the children of all of the Spanish Americas. Why are you disgracing yourself like this?"

"Good day, Ms. Fontana," he says and walks away with his two aides and the rest of the men.

They move down the main aisle and pass Sister Serena. The Assistant Secretary glances at her talking to the boy, but ignores them. Halfway down they hear a commotion and turn.

"Oh my…" The Assistant Secretary and everyone else are shocked.

Sister Serena zips past all of them, six feet in the air on a silver hover-board. People duck as she flies over them and then jumps off it when she reaches the main stage. Security appear from everywhere and rush to the stage.

She is already speaking into the invisible sound zone. "Women, it's 2096 and these men are still trying to shut us up in the Spanish Americas on the issues we care about. All together now." She raises her hands in the air. Everyone notices the illegal cross on the necklace around her neck. "No sex…till no sex slavery."

Some burst out laughing, others are in complete disbelief, but soon all the women in the assembly rise to their feet from their seats, both delegates and citizens, and begin chanting, getting louder and louder.

The Secretary General appears from the side with several aides. His face is distraught, not knowing what to do. He angrily looks at the Assistant Secretary.

Khan takes his seat and watches with a smirk.

"What is it?" his aide asks.

"She's putting on a show."

What do you mean?"

"The imaginary god believers run circles around my truth-thinking atheist people, but to watch you'd have to say they are more superior than us."

"I don't know what you mean, sir. What show?"

"Misdirection. I remember when I was in Venezuela when these imaginary god believers played their tricks with the government. Keep us occupied with the left hand, while they do something else with the right. I've seen them do it before."

The shouts by all the women get louder in unison. "No sex until no sex slavery!"

Jungle location, Brazil
2:50 p.m., 1 October 2096

Under the thick tree cover and anti-satellite camouflage nets, dozens of armed men in black military uniforms wait. Some sit in all-terrain vehicles; others stand around three large army-green helicopter personnel carriers.

A man stands up from his passenger seat in one of the Jeeps, gesturing to the men. He continues to listen carefully to the messages coming though his ear-set communicator.

"We move! Move out now!" he yells in Portuguese. "The military is coming."

The men rush to the heli-transports and board as the Jeeps

drive to the rear of the transports' opening cargo bay doors and then inside. In moments, they are airborne.

"This is the Brazilian Armed Forces. Unidentified transports, you are to immediately reverse your ascent and land," a male voice booms through the overhead of each transport.

The uniformed men ignore it. In the cockpit of the lead heli-transport, the senior man gestures to the pilots. They increase their upward velocity.

"This is the Brazilian Armed Forces. You will be fired upon—"

"Brazilian military," a female voice interrupts him on the same frequency. "You will not fire upon those transports. They are filled with illegal sex slaves. You will stand down and return to your base."

"Who is this? Get off this channel. You are not to interfere with official military operations."

"Brazilian military, stand down or we will open fire on *you*."

"Who is this?"

"This is the military forces of the Underground Railroad. The slaves on those transports will be liberated. The slavers will be captured or killed. Any interference from you will be dealt with by deadly force."

The men in the transports look at each other with worried looks. The boss man touches his ear-set to talk.

"This is the captain of the transport. No one fire on us. We are transporting legal cargo."

"Captain of the unidentified transports," the male voice says, "we have been tracking your Jeep convoy for the last two hours and we tracked your three heli-transports as soon as they entered Brazilian airspace. We scanned the transports and you have six thousand persons in your cargo holds. You are to land immediately."

"Captain," the female voice says, "my sister and I are going to slice your head off and give it to the children to play football with in the streets."

"Underground Railroad, get off this channel!" the male voice yells.

"Captain, we will be face-to-face soon," she says.

The captain looks at his men. "Where are they?"

"We don't see anything in the air," a man in the cockpit answers, his eyes fixed on his display console. "And nothing is on radar."

"Find them. How far is the military?"

"They're in target range now."

Three jets close in on the four heli-transports. From within the clouds, a volley of laser tracer missiles strike. The lead Brazilian military jet's tail bursts into fire and the wings of the second and third erupt. All three spiral down into jungles below. Multiple eject seats shoot away into the sky as the jets explode on impact.

The rotary blades of the heli-transports are hit next. The sky-ships rapidly descend as spoiler wings automatically pop out from the sides. The four transports crash violently through the tree canopy to the ground.

The uniformed slave runners exit the transports or fall out. The captain hops on his left leg out of the lead ship and gestures to his men.

"Set up defense positions now! Make the perimeter farther into the jungle."

The captain is shot first. Gunfire erupts from within the trees. After a few moments, bipedal robot 'hounds' exit the jungle and run to the bodies of the dead uniformed men scattered everywhere. They scan each body for life signs. One man is alive and the robot fires a round from its face turret into his head, killing him. The hounds power down to stand-by mode.

Heavily armed men and women in camouflaged uniforms come out of the jungle towards the transports. They all are wearing green tinted goggles and swarm around the area, re-scanning for any bio or heat signatures. The fighters speak Spanish to each other.

The Twins appear with a bodyguard detail of fighters. Their code name used to be The Betty Boop Twins for their fascination and unique slicked-back hairstyles from the 1940s cartoon character of the same name. Now it is simply The Twins. They are the 'conductors' of the slave rescue operation. Their belts have a gun holster each, but most prominent is the various kinds of knives lining it. Around their necks on a chain is also a dagger each.

"Notify Archangel that the packages have been secured," one of the Twins says to a squad member.

"Yes, ma'am."

As the comm person starts to call in, a female and male team run to them.

"Multiple casualties," he says.

One Twin asks, "Are we secure?"

"One secure," a voice comes in through her ear-set.

"Two, secure," a new voice says.

"Three, secure."

"Four, secure."

The Twins turn to look at another member of their squad. The squad member looks up from her wrist display and says, "No approaching military on the board."

"That won't remain the case for long," one Twin says.

The other Twin says into her ear-set line, "We need Med Corps in here now. Multiple packages have been damaged."

"Touching down now," a female voice responds.

Two sky-ships appear above them, hovering. They begin to

descend slowly. As the wind whips up dirt and debris, its doors begin to open. The first person to jump off is Rabba Silva, even before the Amish and Mennonite men can help her. She's wearing a white headscarf and a white apron with a large Star of David over her casual black dress attire. Silva is one of the few female rabbis in the Orthodox Jewish Order and the mission's medical operational leader. She counts each person of the initial line of Amish and Mennonite men as they jump onto the ground. The Amish men wear dark denim pants, a light blue shirt with the sleeves rolled up, and suspenders, with their wide-brimmed straw hats. The Mennonite men have blue denim overalls over their dark-colored shirts and wear black fedoras. For both Orders, men don't shave their beards after they marry and never allow mustaches to grow. None of the men have beards. Silva begins to count the Christian women (Amish, Mennonite, and Catholic nuns) and Jewish women (Hasidic and Orthodox) as they exit the gunship too. Amish women are in standard dress—hair worn in a bun under white bonnets, long-sleeved calf-length blue dresses, black shoes, and stockings. Mennonite women dress similar to Amish women, but wear wide-brimmed hats.

The Twins walk to Rabba Silva, but wait until she finishes counting. The juxtaposition of Amish, Mennonite, and Old World Jews, all whose dress hadn't changed in some two hundred years on high-tek sky-ships with robots running about still elicits slight amusement in the Twins. The Medical Corps teams quickly move to the transports.

"How many are there?" Rabba Silva asks.

"Six thousand," one Twin answers.

"Offensive. How many millennia have to pass before this evil institution is no more?" Rabba Silva says, shaking her head.

"How is your team doing?"

"My girls and my boys are all doing splendid. I see the new Medical Corps as being a permanent structure within the Continuum. Don't you agree?"

"I don't know why we didn't do it sooner," a Twin says.

"We need to be out of here yesterday," her sister says.

Rabba Silva nods. "We will have the uninjured board your helicopters and the wounded on ours. Not quite in time for yesterday, but in time for fifteen to twenty minutes from now."

The Twins smile.

"Thank you, Rabba," they say.

"Thank you, Sisters," Silva answers back.

The Twins are formally the Sisters Guerras, senior leaders in the New Catholic Order.

"You'll be back in time to see that nice young man of yours made pope," Silva adds.

"We'll save you a seat."

Inside the transport is like a massive cattle car, virtually dark except for the dim glow of red lights above. The women are shackled, row after row of benches. They all sit quietly with all eyes on the main cargo doors—tired, ragged, shaken, and scared. They had heard the explosions outside. Their own transport practically crashed vertically to the ground.

The massive rear cargo hold door begins to open—retracting away and down. A couple of the women jump up from their benches and run to the sides of the opening bay door for cover—they have broken free from their shackles due to the crash. The door is about halfway down when the figure of the first man approaches. One of the women raises with both hands what looks to be a giant dome metal nut and slams it down on the man's head as soon as he sets a foot inside. The man falls forward to the ground.

The door is completely open and with the full light, the women can see that it is actually a surrogate robot. Outside are several more and behind them are real men and women in camo-fatigues. Behind them are strangely dressed men with wide-brimmed hats and women in bonnets.

"Hey!" a woman's voice in English says. The Amish woman tries to walk forward, but is restrained by the Amish men and the soldiers. "Why isn't this working?" she asks one of the soldiers. One of the women soldiers pushes the button on the small device clipped to her dress. "Testing," she says in English.

"Testing," the translator repeats in Portuguese.

"That's better," she says with the device repeating.

"Hey! I said. Why did you knock over our robot?" She looks at the soldiers. "I keep telling you that your robots look too mean. You need to make fluffy robots."

The soldiers smile and laugh.

Kristiana returns her attention back to the women. "We're the good guys, so put down that weapon. I'm Kristiana of the Amish Order. Do you know about us?"

The device repeats her words.

The woman drops the metal component and it crashes to the metal floor with an echoing thud. She nods.

"My friends here are Catholics, Mennonites, Hasidim, Orthodox, and other Amish like me. We're here to help you. These soldiers are going to check everything inside first and then release all your restraints. Then you'll come with us," Kristiana says. "We're the Underground Railroad."

"They don't know what that is," says one of the male soldiers. "Underground Railroad is the northern term—from America, Mexico, and Canada. Say 'The Invisible Fighters.' That's the term here. It's short for 'The Fighters for Invisible Women.'"

"Oh," she says. The device repeats exactly, making her smile. "We're the Fighters for Invisible Women."

All the women stand after the translator repeats.

"That got their attention," Kristiana says. "And we're the Medical Corps. We'll make sure you're safe and medically well. Then we'll take you to your homes. You're free. Is that okay?"

The women nod; some begin to cry.

"Kristiana, for a pacifist you're very bold," says one of the Orthodox Jewish women. "I'd say it's a good thing you're a pacifist."

"I told her when she was in my classes that she was a pacifist with the warrior's heart," Rabba Silva says.

She smiles at her. "I don't know about that. I like to get to things and cut out all the nonsense. I think that's the best way. And these women need us to be that way for them now."

The Catholic fighters have every bay door open on all three of the heli-transports and closely watch both the area and the surrounding jungle. The Medical Corps of Amish, Mennonite, Catholic, and Jewish women use hover-gurneys to move the more seriously wounded of the women; others help or lead the able to the two medical sky-ships. Amish and Mennonite men stay close to give a sense of security, keeping an active watch of the surroundings. Most of the women are scantily dressed, all are young, and none of them have seen daylight or food for days.

"Movement!" one of the watchers yells, looking up from her wrist display.

Everyone moves faster. A squad member snaps her fingers and the robot hounds re-activate and run back into the jungle.

"Everyone is aboard," a squad member says to the Twins.

They see Rabba Silva step back onto her lead med-ship and give the Twins a thumbs up signal.

The Twins nod and lead the remaining Catholic fighter squads back into the jungle.

Two new Brazilian military gun-ships slow to a stop above the jungle. Multiple tracer missiles strike and explode both helicopters, with eject seats launching. The convoy appears from under the trees—seven hover-jets of the Underground Railroad and the two Med Corps med-ships—and rocket away as the pilots of the destroyed military gun-ships parachute down as fragments and debris rain down to the ground.

The Palácio do Planalto, Brasília, Brazil
7:50 p.m., 1 October 2096

The Brazilian president listens to the briefing of his men.

"They wiped out every remaining slave-running cartel," the aide says. "It was nothing short of a full-scale extermination."

"How?" the president asks. "Do we know for certain it was them? Did they have outside military help?"

"They don't even try to hide it anymore," his general says. "They identified themselves as Invisible Fighters. Our aircraft were shot from the sky with advanced weaponry—Mexican weaponry and aircraft. Mexican military illegally operating within our borders, on our soil."

"Classic strategy. They hit when the OAS was in session knowing that the bulk of our ground and air forces would be occupied there protecting all the member state delegates."

"Do you have the proof it was Mexican military?" the president asks.

"Mr. President, it must have been them."

"These Invisible Fighters—"

"The Fighters for Invisible Women. They go by the name Underground Railroad in Mexico," an aide interjects.

"These Invisible Fighters have been operating for years without anyone's military. Quite successfully. There have been independent groups operating in Central America and South American long before Mexico got involved in this…what do they call it?"

"The Slave Wars," another aide answers.

"Why do you want to bring Mexico into this?" the president asks.

"Mexico is running it all now. The whole country is run by these religious zealots. Their secular puppet government is for show. Their lead church-man is selecting the government all over the country."

"Do you have the proof of any of this, General?"

The general starts to say something, but stops.

"Tensions between Mexico and Brazil have been bad since before we were born. No one in this room likes Mexico, but I want proof before we go to war with Mexico or any other nation in the Spanish Americas. Our cold war with Mexico existed long before their church people rose to recent power. The United States is not religious and they are not our ally. The CHINs are atheistic too, but they are not our allies either. I am not into the atheists are our friends and the religious are our enemies. We are not children. You tell me the Mexican president is a puppet of the religious church-people. Others tell me he is the puppet of the United States. General, get me proof. "

"Sorry, Mr. President. I stepped out of line. We're tired of the Mexicans. We all know Mexico is involved in everything. Trying to be like the United States used to be. Meddling in other countries' business. We're fighting these slave wars too. It is

Brazilian women being snatched by these global gangsters. They have no right to trespass into our land. We're tired of the Mexicans and Argentineans undercutting our sovereignty and diminishing our standing to be a global superpower. We should be running all of the Spanish Americas."

"We will soon, but one must be patient. We must be ready. Do we want what happened to the Russians to happen here? Their president got himself assassinated. We stay in the shadows a bit longer. Grow our power quietly."

"Yes, Mr. President."

"Sir, we may not be able to prove the Mexican government was directly involved, but we do know the Invisible Fighters are based in Mexico and their leader is Mexican. This religious gangster named Marcos and these Mexicans feel they can invade anyone's airspace to rescue slaves, more like prostitutes."

One of the military men looks at his palm device as the Brazilian president says to them, "Get me the Mexican president on the line. Let's see what he has to say."

One of the aides rushes out of the room.

"Mr. President," the officer with the palm device says, "I think you need to see this."

The president takes the device and plays the vid-message. He recognizes the man as one of the leading South American cartel bosses.

"Make sure your boss, President Jimenas himself, sees this, General. We had an arrangement—the cartels and the government. You stay out of our business; we keep the jihadis off the Spanish American continent. That was the arrangement. Hasn't it worked out well for everyone? No chance of the Spanish Americas ever going Muslim. Now you're reneging on that arrangement. It's fine with us because we're not scared of them and we're okay with a never-ending war with them. I always prefer target practice with live humans. When they come for your heads, don't come to us to save you. Choose your allies wisely, my father taught me. You have chosen unwisely. And, if you're going to go after our slave-running business, it might be wise to keep to your wives and sex-bots and not be buying slaves yourselves. Why are politicians always such hypocrites?"

Near Mexico City, Mexico
2:30 a.m., 28 September 2096

Augustín is fast asleep when the steady beeping of the phone rouses him. His wife, next to him, slowly sits up in the bed. He opens his eyes fully. The room has a faint blue glow from the night light.

"I'll get it," he says. "Go back to sleep." She lies back down and covers herself with the blanket. "Who is it for?" he calls out to the computer.

"Official call for Deputy Director of the Secretariat of Public Security, Señor Augustín."

He walks out of the bedroom and closes the door behind him. He grabs the ear-set from the general table and puts it in his right ear. "Augustín," he says as he walks into the living room.

"Sorry to disturb you, sir."

"What is it?"

"We have a situation."

"With?"

"The Presidential Palace."

He notices the time on one of the wall clocks. 2:31 am. "How upset will I be?"

"The president is secretly organizing a special legislative session for next Tuesday."

"Why are you calling me about politics?"

"It is a security and intelligence matter, sir. He has scheduled a general meeting for a specific time, but has the entire Parliament secretly under arrest for fear of leaks."

"What time?"

"Noon."

Augustín remains quiet.

"Do you know what that time signifies?"

"Keep a close eye on everyone and everything. I will get back with you."

"Yes, sir."

He disconnects the line and briskly walks into another room and closes the door.

Private Landing Field, Sinaloa, Mexico
7:10 a.m., 29 September 2096

Niccolo disembarks from a white hover-jet as the steps lower to the ground. He is dressed in a full black office suit, his shirt only buttoned halfway. He is in his late forties with green eyes and is naturally bald.

Two men stand near a waiting SUV as he approaches.

"Niccolo, you have a call," one of his guards says as the Italian is getting into the limousine.

He gets in and throws his jacket across the open seats. He touches his ear-set as he activates his private e-pad. It is Augustín's face.

"The Mexican insider," he says.

"The Italian fixer," Augustín says.

"You never call me, so this must be important."

"What happens at twelve noon today?"

Niccolo pauses for a moment.

"Niccolo, send your men to pick me up at my house now. Hurry."

New Lerdo Church, New Lerdo City, Durango, Mexico
9:00 p.m., 30 September 2096

The Catholic Continuum are meeting in the church's Executive Meeting Hall. The senior leadership of all three contingents of the New Catholic Order—Spanish American, African, and Italian—some nearly four dozen people. The room looks like it was carved out of white marble, including the conference table that is in the shape of a "T."

"That means nothing," one of Niccolo's men challenges. The younger Sicilian man is also dressed in black. "Why are we concerned about some Exile Jews who will say anything to get our attention? They're excommunicated so the meeting should never have happened."

"That is true," Mona Lisa replies. The slim woman has model-like features with olive skin and silky black hair styled to hang to the right side of her face. She wears a basic white sleeveless dress with color matching pearls around her neck, and heels. "But the Continuum had other reasons for allowing the exception."

"Meaning?" one of the nun leaders asks. "These Exiles are all government spies. They don't even deny it. That's why they were excommunicated. Why did the Jewish Continuum allow the meeting?"

"And I hear that the Protestants have also allowed meetings with their Exiles," a senior deacon says. "And don't say it's because we want to be compassionate to their children who were born or were little when they were excommunicated."

"It will be discussed at the Full Continuum meeting," Mona Lisa assures them.

"But you know why?" a nun asks.

"Yes."

"Do you concur with the decision?"

"I do."

"Brethren," the large face of Archbishop Masai from Africa stares back at them from the vid-screen in the center of the room, "is this a matter for the Catholic Continuum or is it a matter for our security and intel services until there is more? Is there a threat to Father Marcos? Is there a threat to the ceremony? That's all that concerns me. Niccolo?"

"We have nothing concrete now, Archbishop," Niccolo answers.

"You and I both know that many lives have been saved in our time by not waiting for the concrete. What do your instincts say?" Archbishop Masai asks.

"There could be something, but we must investigate further. I do agree with the sentiment of the group that it is extremely suspicious for a group of Exile Jews sitting in Florida with supposedly no contact with Faith World to have any knowledge at all of the ceremony. It could be someone within their ranks playing a game with us just to see us chase our tails. But then again, how could they know when not even the general Catholic population knows?"

"We have more security here than has ever been assembled before by any Faither community in our history," Mr. Blond, the ex-Texas Catholic, says. "No one and nothing of any kind will get near Father Marcos that's not supposed to."

"My Lost Boys will tell us if anything is wrong," young Rodrigo speaks up. The boy is an official leader in the Catholic Continuum too. "There's nothing. No chatter."

"We did wipe out the final remnants of the slavers in Brazil," a priest says. "Could there be a connection? Cartel retaliation?"

"There's no one left to retaliate," Sister Serena answers. "The women were liberated back to their families. But again, no one outside our Continuum knows. No one in Brazil or any Spanish America government, including Mexico, knows. The other Faither Continuums didn't learn of it until weeks ago."

"When was the official Papal Conclave?" Mr. Blond asks.

"Last December," Archbishop Masai answers. "But the College of Cardinals is only twelve people, including myself. Security preparations were made for the ceremony without participants even knowing they were doing so for the ceremony. The Catholic Continuum was only informed recently."

"Do we really believe it's even remotely possible that there was a leak within our Continuum?" Mona Lisa asks. "I don't believe that for a moment. It must be something else. These are Exiles. Liars."

"Agreed," Masai says. Other Continuum members nod.

"Didn't these Exile Jews have this information long before our final Brazilian operations?" Serena asks.

"Yes," one of the men answers.

"So the timelines don't even match," Serena notes.

"I'll continue to investigate," Niccolo says.

"We should all simply do our jobs as normal. We'll leave it to the real secret agents like Niccolo to find out if anything nefarious is really being plotted," Mona Lisa says. "In addition to the normal plots we have to contend with."

"If I could see Niccolo and Augustín alone after we adjourn," the Archbishop says.

The group says their goodbyes and adjourns. Masai's face disappears from the screens. When everyone else is gone from the room, Masai's face reappears. Niccolo and Augustín are the only ones remaining.

"Mr. Augustín," Masai says.

"Yes, Archbishop."

"You were very quiet."

"I talk when there is something to say."

"Could this all be tied to the information you shared with Father Marcos? The Bull, the Turtle, the Lion."

Augustín thinks for a moment.

"No one knows that I know."

"But others suspect too," Niccolo adds.

"Suspicions mean little in intelligence and politics," Augustín says. "There are always suspicions. You must have the smoking gun."

"But you did decide to share these suspicions with Father Marcos," Masai says, "and as a result of that conversation, Mexico will soon have a new president by our own machinations behind the scenes. You knew this would be the result of that conversation."

"Father Marcos has many enemies. The Continuum has many enemies," Niccolo says.

"But they don't know we know," Augustín says. "We haven't moved against them and we've made no indications that we are or that we will ever move against them. I appreciate the adage that 'a paranoid people never die,' but even our paranoia can become crazy."

"Perhaps," Masai says.

"Archbishop," Niccolo says, "we will get to the bottom of it either way. Mr. Elliott will follow the leads with the Exiles directly. He's taking point on their One Project for both the Jewish and Protestant Orders. We'll pursue the matter from our own angles. If there is a real plot, we'll find it."

"I have every confidence in you, Niccolo," Masai says. "You saved our future pope once. I know you can do so again."

New Lerdo Church, New Lerdo City, Durango, Mexico
6:50 a.m., 2 October 2096

Church services of the Catholic Order are earlier than any of the Christian Orders. The attendance today will be massive and it will be broadcast via Freespace to Faith World sites all over the Spanish Americas, Africa, and the rest of the world. Local townspeople fill every inch of the streets to the church. Young and old, all smiling and happy faces, eager and anxious for the start of the new city's celebration that is being called the city's official 'christening.' Every road on the outer perimeter of the city has been barricaded to all vehicles so even the invited dignitaries—elected officials, Catholic leaders from surrounding territories, prominent businesspeople— are on foot too.

Over three years ago, it was a meager, run-down church—until Father Marcos arrived. Now the rebuilt church is a unique, stark-white structure like the old cathedral Sacre Coeur in Paris, France before the Islamic occupation. Actually, it is the second version of New Lerdo Church—three times the size of the previous one and the parish grounds are five times larger, not including the expanded living quarters and garden; all courtesy of one of the trillionaire families of Mexico.

Among the crowds, moving through the people and watching without being noticed, are Lost Boys, from as young as six to sixteen. The term was always the term for orphaned or abandoned boys that used to loiter Mexican streets, but Father Marcos in particular, and now the entire Catholic Order in Mexico and many parts of the Spanish Americas, gave them permanent homes, found them jobs, and gave them purpose. The Lost Boys, unknown to most outside New Lerdo City, are also the New Catholic Order's primary street surveillance and informants. Here in the Spanish Americas the threat to Faithers is the government and the cartels.

Human intelligence, not who has the most guns or the best tek, is the bedrock of their defense. If something is happening or going to happen on the streets of Durango, the Lost Boys will be the first to know.

Niccolo and Augustín are among the many people walking to the church. A Lost Boy glances at them, sitting on a window sill of a bordering closed business establishment and waves hello. It is Rodrigo. Not even a teen yet, but not only an official member of the Catholic Continuum's senior leadership, but the leader of all the Lost Boys—and Lost Girls. The men gesture back.

Augustín notices that there are many newborns among the crowd.

"Are there going to be baptisms too?"

Niccolo nods. "Yes, a special day for them. All of them. And then…that little thing happens."

Augustín grins. "Are half the people here undercover security?"

"No, Augustín. More like three-quarters."

As they come over the hill, they have an unobstructed view of the road to the church. There seems to be millions of people walking to it. And there on the hill, high above, is the church. They saw it before, but from this vantage point it looks like it is floating above the ground—an amazing construction. To think not too long ago the entire area had to be destroyed and rebuilt because of a narco-cartel plot and…scorpions.

People already treat New Lerdo as the new Vatican, but most, even within Catholicism, have no idea that it is—Rome fell to Caliphate years ago, a secret maintained by both Faithers and the Caliphate in the know.

"Who's waiting for us?" Augustín asks.

"Everyone, but we cannot burden him with this. We must handle it. He has the baptism service and the other things to occupy his mind."

Niccolo realizes just how many babies there really are in the crowds. Some being held by their fathers, others in their mother's arms, some by older siblings, others sitting in front pouches of either parent. What's odd to him is that none of the babies are crying.

"The babies. They are all, collectively, so well-behaved. Did you drug them?" he asks.

"You're Italian so you wouldn't understand," Augustín replies. "Mexican babies are the best behaved newborns in the world."

"No, that's Italian babies. I think you're drugging them."

The men's joking around continues as they near the small wall surrounding the main grounds of the church. Both men see the White Guardsmen first—Texas Catholics who abandoned America to be the dedicated security force for the New Mexican Catholic leader. In the front, greeting the townspeople, are the church's primary and volunteer staff of nuns, priests, deacons, and lay volunteers. They follow the crowds under the small archway when Niccolo sees the man he is expecting.

7:25 a.m.

Niccolo arrives at the internal command center for New Vatican— everyone uses the phrase nowadays. The man-made hill where the official offices and residences sit was hollowed out for the many floors of the secret command center. Ironically, the Day of the Scorpion event gave them the idea.

He is offered a chair by staff but tells them he prefers to stand. The Watching Room is an enormous vid-cam surveillance center, row after row, station after station manned by security men and women in white office suits. Like the Tek World they fled, all

Faither cities have the same surveillance systems of stationary vid-cams and drones for security.

Niccolo glances at each monitor in view. Every inch of New Lerdo City is monitored in real-time, outside and in every building—even the hall of the main ten-thousand-seat church where people eagerly await Father Marcos to begin the special 7:30 a.m. services. People continue to gather who can't get inside the church or prefer to be outside and watch the services on the outside vid-screens. He notices the White Guardsmen (visible security) stationed at entrances and other key points, Lost Boys—and Lost Girls—in the crowds (semi-concealed security), and knows that there are many more undercover security personnel. He walks over to another set of monitor banks and sees the feed from the city's own drones.

"Sir," says a man sitting closest to him. "Nothing will happen to the pope today. He survived many years against the cartels without us. Now he has us to see to his protection."

Niccolo smiles and pats him on the shoulder. "I'm Sicilian. I can't help myself."

"I'm Duranguese—People of the Scorpion. We're the same."

They watch the Christening Ceremony begin on the monitors. At the front interior of the church are an army of parents waiting with their newborns. The stage has been modified to have its own pool along the entire width. Father Marcos appears on the stage from a side entrance. He is a clean-cut young man in his late thirties, dressed in an all white cassock with matching white sash, white kippot on his head, and a large golden cross around his neck on a chain. This Mexican "city boy" single-handedly created the Mexican Underground Railroad and saved Catholicism from cartel and government alike in the country to become its religious leader.

He immediately greets the congregation with a humble, "Good

morning, fellow children of God." He has never gotten used to it and doesn't care for it, but the crowd erupts in applause. After a few minutes, he raises his arms to settle down the people and says, "Let us pray." This day of baptism is also their annual Memorial of the Guardian Angels holiday.

Father Marcos begins with ritual prayers, but his words in Spanish are far from rote. The emotion in his tone is genuine, as if he is uttering them for the first time. The Italian members of the congregation wear translator ear-set devices in their ears. When he finishes the official prayer service, a nun and deacon appear on either side of him as he motions to the families with their newborns to step onto the stage in front of the pool. The nun hands him his Bible.

"Do we have any dignitaries in the congregation this morning?" Niccolo asks.

"Yes," one of the Watchers answers. "The Governor and his family are here. Representatives from the Presidential Palace always attend—"

"To spy," Niccolo interjects.

"Of course, and we have representatives from three other states too."

Father Marcos continues reading from his Bible before handing it back to the nun and stepping into the pool. The first line of families does the same—all dressed in their Sunday finest, shoes and all. The overhead speaker broadcasts his exchange with the families asking their names and where they are from. Father Marcos begins the baptisms, one-by-one, carefully taking the newborns from the parents in his arms, asking the parents their full name, repeating it as he blesses them, covering their nose and mouth as he gently submerges them beneath the water. He lifts them up and hands them back to their parents. Some of the babies immediately begin to cry afterward, others remain calm. The ceremony will take hours, and more nuns and deacons join him in the pool to help with the queue.

8:15 a.m.

A heavy-set man stumbles up the cobblestone road, sweating abnormally and out of breath. He looks up at the sun as he shields his eyes, and then stops his walk towards the church. People around him notice his state, but keep moving. The man touches his chest, goes down to one knee, and then falls to the ground. People immediately run to help him.

9:11 a.m.

They continue to watch the ceremony. Father Marcos may be only asking three simple questions of each family, but he does so in a way to sincerely engage with each one. Every spectator, whether in the church, outside watching from the monitors, or Niccolo and the others in the command center, are completely immersed in the ceremony.

"Do you believe it's already been over ninety minutes, Mr. Niccolo?" a Watcher says to him.

Niccolo nods. "I can almost recite the names of each baptized child myself."

"Yes."

"When will the Feast of the Guardian Angels begin?"

"Noon, sir."

Another hour passes before Father Marcos finishes his last baptism. He steps out of the pool, and instead of drying himself with the towel a deacon hands him, he drapes it around his neck. The nuns and the deacons step back and exit from the stage as cardinals and bishops—Mexican, other Spanish American, Italian, and African—dressed in red with white collars, take to the stage. They form a semi-circle around Father Marcos.

The lead cardinal stands out in the center of the group—Cardinal Cassiano. He is a well-built man in his fifties. An imposing stature of six foot three, with perfectly tan skin, a clean-shaven face, and sophisticated, styled, graying hair. He seems more suited for the role of an actor or billionaire playboy than a church-man. But the Italian is one of the major movers-and-shakers within the Catholic universe. Archbishop Masai is the "General" of the Catholic Order—maintaining the victory and peace on the African continent against the Caliphate, but Cardinal Cassiano is called the "Chairman," by Catholic clergy—a reference to his insatiable love of the music of the twentieth-century actor and singer, Frank Sinatra, but really speaks to his status within the church hierarchy itself, before and after the Fall of Vatican Rome. He is the Administrator of the Catholic Order.

The families are all back at their seats and no one in the congregation quite knows what is happening. More Catholic dignitaries take to the stage as two priests in black walk to Father Marcos with new clothing and help him into a new white and gold cassock.

Cardinal Cassiano steps forward and says in Italian, "My fellow brothers and sisters in Christ, we in the Catholic Order have been carrying a heavy burden, this secret of ours. Today that burden will be lifted and our limbo will be at an end."

Niccolo takes notice of a man and woman walking to him across the floor.

"Mr. Niccolo," she says, "you wanted to be informed of any anomalies, no matter how small."

"Yes."

"A townsman on the way to the church collapsed."

"From what?"

"Heat exhaustion. He's being attended to by medics."

"Can I see the feed?"

"Yes, of course."

They lead him to another set of monitor banks and on multiple screens are different angles of two medics attending to the man. He is sitting on the ground and a medic is getting him to drink more water. Another medic continues to read his bios with her hand scanner.

"What is protocol in this situation?"

"He'll be taken to the hospital."

"If he wants to continue to the church?"

"There's no room at all, so it will be at one of the external monitors. We'll allow it if he wants to."

"Anything strange?"

"Nothing at all. We're checking everything, his ID, calling his home, bio-scans, everything. On this day of all days, we're not interested in any anomalies either."

"Did you notify the Continuum too?"

"Yes, and Archbishop Masai personally."

Suddenly all the lights of the Watching Room turn red and low sirens start bleeping. Everyone on the floors stands, looking up at the lights and at each other.

"Keep at your posts!" floor wardens yell throughout the floor.

Archbishop Masai's face appears on every screen. "This is a priority red alert. There is a man suffering from apparent heat exhaustion being attended to by medics. He is not—I repeat—not to be allowed into the church's inside perimeter. Deadly force is sanctioned."

10:16 a.m.

The man is still somewhat winded. "I'm feeling better," the man says.

"Are you sure, sir?" the female medic asks.

"Yes. I'm going to go back home. It must have been something I ate."

He stands to his feet, takes the bottle of water from the medic, turns, and starts back along the path he came.

"Get better, sir," the male medic says.

"You can watch the ceremony on your local broadcast channel at home," the female medic adds.

"Thank you," he says, lifting his hand in the air, walking without turning to look at them.

The medics gather their kits, start back to the church, and stop. White Guardsmen descend from the sky wearing rocket-packs with guns drawn. Multiple drones also appear, hovering in the sky.

"Where is he?" one of the White Guardsman asks in Spanish with his Texas accent.

"Who? The sick man? He went home."

The Guardsmen jump and fly away to where she pointed. More Guardsmen appear in the sky and follow.

People both inside the Church and those watching the monitors outside are overwhelmed by emotion, all taken by surprise. Father Marcos stands before a congregation on its feet, wildly applauding and cheering, and the cardinals and bishops stand behind him clapping. Marcos Agustin de Arango is the new pope—the pope for the Catholic Order all over the world to lead them into the next century. *Pope Marcos I.*

The Hand of the Five Cities of the Plain

The Ant-Hill, Unknown Location, America
9:03 a.m., 9 October 2096

A secret desert location in the American Trog-land territories. A colossal underground facility that few Faithers know its true location, including the state it's in. Attendees are transported in by land or air in craft without any way to ascertain direction or distance.

The Catholic Order has Mr. Blond and the White Guardsmen. The African Collective has the Catholic Masai Warriors. The Jewish Orders have Shoshana and the Wolf Pack. The Protestants have Sek, short for "security," and the Templars for their elite security.

Sek is taller than average height with a slim, muscular build, brown eyes, and close-cropped hair. He always makes rounds before any high-level meeting, early in the morning and alone. It is his time for quiet reflection before the bustle of the day begins. But today is not just any high-level meeting—it is the full Continuum. The Protestants, Catholics, Jews, Mormons, Anabaptists, Shogun,

Magi, and African Collective. The formal alliance of the 'superpowers' of the Faith World.

The Continuum had the Ant-Hill built specifically for these types of meetings. Sek demanded it, feeling the round-robin approach of having random enclaves host the meetings was too dangerous, and continuous holo-meetings in Freespace was not the proper venue for the strategic meetings that the Faithers needed to happen on a fairly regular basis.

Deeply devout himself, religiosity must always remain secondary to the safety of the people. March and April are the High Holy Days for Protestant Christians. September and October are the High Holy Days for Jews. Catholics and Mormons are split with April and December, as are the Amish and Mennonites. Shinto and Magi follow the Protestant days. Five months when no Continuum meetings happen, but past mid-October there is a window of availability. The Jewish Order's Simchat Torah is today and their members will arrive tomorrow.

Continuum members began arriving yesterday, but the official meeting won't commence until tomorrow. He wishes they didn't need to have the Ant-Hill. The whole weight of the world is on his shoulders. He reflects on the days when he was chief of security for just one enclave, then all the sister enclaves in their region, until he moved up the security and intel ranks to his current position. All of the leadership in one place on this day and his responsibility, along with the Templars under his command, to keep every last man, woman, and child safe.

He walks into the command center offices. No sooner does he appear when several of his staff see him and race to him. He holds up his hand.

"May I get my coffee first?"

His smiling assistant appears behind him. "Here you are, sir."

He returns the smile as he takes the cup. Before they can barrage him, he holds up his hand again as he downs the coffee.

"Okay, I'm ready for the onslaught now."

"Sir, Mr. Niccolo of the Catholic Order is waiting in your office."

"Okay."

"Sir, the Mormon Order wants to have a private meeting with you first before their meeting with the Executive Quorum."

"Okay. And?"

"The Underground Railroad is waiting for you in your other office, sir."

"Okay."

"Sir, your son is waiting for you in your other private office."

"My son? What happened?"

"Nothing, sir. He wanted to come by and check on you."

"Check on me?" Sek says with an amused surprise.

The female staffer turns to the others. "His son had his Bar Barakah yesterday."

The group congratulate him. Jews had bar-mitzvahs. Christians' coming of age ceremonies, or Bar Barakahs, had become as common ever since the Separatist Movement almost three decades ago. They are family ceremonies, partly religious, for teenage boys and girls to give meaning to their transition from childhood to adulthood. Always a significant life event, but because of preparation for the Continuum meeting, Sek could not attend. But his family had it recorded for him.

"Okay. Son first. Mormons next. Railroad afterward. Mr. Niccolo last, since I know it will take the longest."

10:28 a.m.

Sek comes out of the office side by side with his son.

"I'm going to hug you while I still have the chance. You're fifteen now, so soon you won't want to be in the same room as your mother and me."

"Father, that's not true."

He gives his son a hug and looks at him. "A man."

"Oh, leave me alone."

"What are you going to do today?"

"I have my atmospheric engineering classes."

"I don't know what that is, but I'm sure you're good at it. Off to class."

"See you later, Father. You can wake me up if you get home before midnight."

"Are you sure?"

"Yes. I don't need as much sleep as old-timers like you."

"Old-timers? Always remember you're right behind us."

His son laughs as he walks to a couple of other boys waiting.

"Hi, Mr. Sek," says one of the boys, who's as tall as Sek.

"Hi, J.J.," he responds. "Hi Daniel."

"Hi, Mr. Sek."

"Keep my son out of trouble."

"He's a man now," J.J. says. "Men don't get in trouble, but just the same, don't tell my parents you saw me."

Sek laughs as the boys wave and walk off.

10:33 a.m.

Sek walks into the private room. "Mr. Vincent."

He shakes the senior Mormon leader's hand and hand of the woman with him. "Ms. River."

"Mr. Sek," they both say.

"Let's sit," he says to them.

Vincent, like Archbishop Masai of the African Collective, is the "supreme general" of all civilian military and intel forces in the Mormon Order, reporting directly to their Fifteen Apostles—First Presidency and Quorum of Twelve Apostles. You would never know to look at him—calm composure, clean shaven, and brown hair. The brunette, River, one of his "generals," also looks like an average, everyday woman.

The senior Mormon leaders skip the small talk to get to their issues.

"I can relay the information to the Executive Board after the meeting," Sek says.

"The Prophet wants to keep this off the public record due to its sensitive nature for us," Vincent says.

"I completely understand, but if it's the wish of the Mormon Order to expunge any mention of them from the record—"

"We want them expunged from the record *and* all Continuum databases. We want it to be as if they never existed. I'm sure you can appreciate this. It's unthinkable what happened— unprecedented."

"The Protestant Order can easily empathize. We had 'fellow' Christians conspiring with Galerius—Boggs—against our own leaders, our entire people. You had one civil war over days. We had ours over several years."

"Thank you," Vincent says. "That's why we approached your Order to help us."

"I'll have the tek work done this week and contact you when it's finished."

The Mormons nod, pleased.

Continuum Meeting
2:15 p.m., 10 October 2096

The meeting hall for the full Continuum meeting is called Congress Hall. It looks more like a mini coliseum with a large, round, donut hole conference table under a massive dome. Large vid-screens line the walls, hovering above the floor. There is much activity prior to the meeting. Pages (teenage boys and girls) representing all the Orders run around making sure the final preparations are all complete—each one planning to be a representative for their Order when older.

Lunch is over and the members make their way from the dining areas in the adjoining hall to Congress Hall. Leaders, assistants, aides, historical media, and observers enter, a million conversations going on at the same time.

A few Arabic Christians are in debate with a few Amish and Mennonite elders.

"…but now that you have formally joined the Medical Corps, and its success will only continue to grow, we believe it reintroduces the whole juxtaposition of pacifists in enclaves of warriors," one of the Arabic Christians says.

"Pacifist atheists is one thing," the Mennonite man responds, "but a pacifist Believer is quite another. We are born into a world of spiritual war, so even we pacifists are warriors in a way. Non-resistance and not killing is a choice as a way to live. It is not an endorsement of the belief that the opposite is never necessary. The Bible does make that abundantly clear. Use the secular term conscientious objector if that helps. In every war, conscientious objectors played key roles in wars against evil. As are we."

"We are Faithers too," the Amish man says. "This side of paradise the war is without end. It should simply be viewed as a natural part of life."

"And we fight that battle against the enemy together," the other Arabic Christian says.

The Amish Elder adds, "When you all have the same enemy, that tends to unify people."

"Amen."

Yonah enters Congress Hall, and after scanning the crowd for a while, he sees his party. They see him too and wave.

The first man to reach him is wearing a white cowboy hat and extends his hand. "The Cowboy Rabbi in the flesh. Mr. Lariat of the Protestant Order."

The woman next to him has a brown cowboy hat with an American Indian bead necklace around her neck. "Mrs. Runningstar of the Conservative Jewish Order."

Yonah knows of both of them well. They were some of the last non-Goth agents working in Tek World and are actually married to each other—intra-religious marriages are rare in Faith World. Usually, one spouse converts to the religion of the other, but not in their case.

The other men are with the Mormon and Catholic Orders; the women are with the Shinto Order and the African Collective."

"I'm only the Cowboy Rabbi when I have my guns, which, for this meeting, are locked up safe at home."

"So we're creating the Cowboy Coalition," Lariat says.

"Yes, we are. A dedicated tactical team for the entire Continuum. We'll be the advance force to go into action before everyone else. Always training and always ready, but that doesn't by any means suggest we're—to use a very old term—to be cannon fodder. We're just the ones to fire the first shot when needed until the cavalry arrives or for quick strike-and-flight ops. We already have the approval for creation of a full contingent of robots for us."

"Please tell me we'll have robotic horses too," Runningstar says. "Seriously?"

"Why not? Cowboys need their horses."

Lariat smiles. "My wife is an accomplished equestrian. Riding since she was five."

"And with robotic horses, we can all be accomplished equestrians," she says.

Sek arrives with Niccolo. They stand at the doorway and scan the room. They see Moses and his wife M (Emma) talking with a group.

"We'll meet with them afterward," Sek says. "We'll need Tova and Mr. Tova from the Conservative Jewish Order too."

"All of them were involved?"

"It was a joint operation of both Orders. Well, back then we didn't have the protocols we have now for operations. It was simpler back then. If you came at us, we were coming after you."

Niccolo laughs.

"You remember how it was before."

"I do."

Remote Outlands Enclave
3:00 p.m., 10 October 2096

The Outlands are the outermost part of tek-cities—sometimes urban, sometimes rural, but always apart from the main city. That is what its residents preferred despite the scarcity of services and rarity of drone patrols. Sometimes adjoining enclaves were built to be even more exclusive and sheltered from outsiders. This enclave is secretly run by Faithers.

The heli-jet is shuttled into the hanger facility by a giant hover-pad. It glides in and sets down in the center of the landing field.

The 'sky' activates. It looks like the sky, but is actually a holo-image on a dome ceiling. The visitors are cleared for disembarking as the doors open. The forty-plus leaders exit and walk along a dusty path to a single dome dwelling. Some of them look at the dusk sky above and others notice that the entire terrain is a dusty desert plain with nothing else visible but their transport. They can hear the faint sounds of an approaching aircraft, but see nothing. The door of the house is open and a man wearing a silver helmet waves to them with a silly grin on his face.

"My name is…hmmm. Let me think."

Everyone is seated on single couches arranged throughout the large circular living room of the dwelling. The doors to male and female restrooms are visible, which some used before getting settled, as well as the entrance to kitchen-dining area, though the scatterbrained man didn't even offer them any water.

"You don't know your name?" a man asks with a frown.

"Of course I know my name. I'm Pagan Paul. I was trying to remember my speech, but I got distracted." He smiles wide. "This is so great. The Jews get new people. The Protestants and we Gnostics get people too. This is great! It makes me want to blow up something tiny—really tiny."

"I thought you were some type of clown, but clearly you're a crazy person," one woman says.

"I'm not crazy. I'm a character. Crazy people don't have great personal references like I have or put in a position of authority. Don't distract me. I need to remember my speech."

"We don't need any speeches. Just talk to us straight," a man says.

Paul smiles and points to the man. "That was the title of my speech."

"Forget the speech. Just tell us what we need to know. We're humiliated enough. Do you get that?" another woman says.

"Humiliated? Why? You have nothing to be humiliated for."

"Yes, we do. I had a good career in the city and now, only because I happen to believe in God, I have to leave my home and live in these self-segregated communities out in nowhere land, never to return. I still don't know how I was found out."

"We don't live in communities. We live in cities. We have our own cities too. And we're not out in nowhere land. We're beyond the reach of the government, where we can protect ourselves and be left alone. And away from all their wires and brain-melting waves."

"What?"

"Never mind. We're safe. And you can go visiting Tek World whenever you want, though I don't know why you'd ever want to."

"I don't like being told where to live. And I don't like being chased from my home. It ticks me off. I don't want to live behind no walls either!" the woman continues.

Pagan Paul laughs. "What do you think the tek-cities are? They got invisible walls around them. It's no different."

"It is different."

"No, it's not."

"Stop it," a man interrupts. "We're not in kindergarten. Tell us what you need to tell us so we can get this over with."

Pagan Paul takes his silver helmet from his single chair, sets it on the floor, and sits on it. He wraps his arms around his knees. Everyone watches him.

"My name is Pagan Paul and I used to live with the Amish in Old Amish Quarter for almost twenty years before the bad Pagans came after us. That should tell you everything you need to know. If they'd come after pacifists, what chance did you think you would have? Well, I don't believe in God and never have. Probably never will, but I won't live with those Pagans. They're mean and hateful. I thought I'd be the only one of my kind in Faith World—that's what we call it—but I was so happy when I found out there were a bunch like me. The Faithers have their religious Orders and their Continuum—that's their alliance—so we created our own. Agnostic Order seemed kind of clunky, but someone came up with just dropping the "A." We're the Gnostic Order. All the agnostics and pro-Faither atheists in Faith World. I like a simple life, prefer it. In Tek World, you can't go to the bathroom without their tek and the government…always scanning, always listening, doing who knows what to you with their machines and invisible rays. We're better off, I tell you. In a generation or two, you'll start to see the mutations in them."

By now the group is looking at one another. *Is he serious or joking with us?*

"We'll remain Homo sapiens. They'll be Homo stupidus." The group is incredulous. "Their brains will be smaller and so will their IQs because of all the exposure to all the tek contamination."

"Excuse me, but let's get back to the serious stuff," one of the men interrupts.

"I am being serious." Pagan Paul thinks for a moment and then looks at the man, smiling. "Well, I think I am. Sometimes I can't tell myself. Well, we have our own section—"

"Segregation upon segregation," the woman says.

Pagan Paul points at her and says, "You are very negative." He drops his hand. "Most of the Gnostics prefer that, just like the Amish live together, the Mennonites, the Protestants, Jews, Catholics, and so on. However!" Pagan Paul raises his hands in the air and flails them around. "You can live with any group you like. But!" He flails around again. "Since you are new, you would have to live in the Gnostic section and then when people trust you, then you can ask to live with any group you like. How did I do?"

"I can't say that I'm overly impressed," says the woman. "They send a clown to present to us rather than someone serious."

Pagan Paul hops up from the ground. He raises his hands and then walks to the window, pulling back the curtains. He gestures for them to join him. The group slowly rise from their seats and walk over.

"What are we looking at?" the woman asks.

Pagan Paul doesn't look, but says, "The color red."

The group looks and notices a reddish helicopter in the nearby landing area of the enclave.

"What do you see painted on it?"

"Symbols," the woman answers.

"It's Japanese, I believe," a man says.

"The Hidden and Lots like you, talk to me. The Exiles get to talk to them."

"Them who?" the woman asks.

"The Yakuza Fukkatsu." Pagan Paul walks up to the woman, real close. "Do you want to talk to me or them?"

The woman tries to look brave but is visibly nervous. "I'm okay with this current status quo."

Pagan Paul throws up his hands and runs from the window to his silver helmet 'seat.' "Okay, let's finish the presentation. We need to be done by lunch. And my belly will not tolerate lateness."

The group looks at each other and then slowly returns to their seats.

Congress Hall, The Ant-Hill
3:26 p.m., 10 October 2096

The meetings normally start later in the day, often well into night, and then everyone goes home—travel is always at night. The

Continuum meeting is in full swing. The invocation and formal introductions are over. They call it the "donut hole," but it is a large round table with the center cut out, and all the senior Continuum leadership are seated around it. For the Jewish Orders: Conservatives, Orthodox, Shamar, Hasidim, Persians, Arabs, and Judeo-Spanish. The Protestants, who merged all their many denominations into one eight years ago. The Catholics with their Spanish American, Italian, and African contingents. The Mormons, the Shogun (Asian Christians, mostly Japanese), and the Magi. The African Collective; led by the African Catholics and made up of Coptic Christians, Ethiopian Jews, Armenian Christians, and various deists. The Anabaptists; Amish and Mennonites. All assistants, aides, and observers sit in the "coliseum" around the seated leaders, in successive rows with one row higher than the row before it, the entire seating area forming a circle. When the main deliberations occur, the section can move to a semi-circle configuration to be addressed by speakers.

On the side walls are other parties sitting and watching, not officially part of the Continuum. Goths (both Jews and Christians) never were an Order, but a coalition—with their spiky black hair, lipstick and eyeshadow, black clothes, and black boots. Their sole purpose is to gather intelligence from within the tek-cities and blend in with the population. Gnostics—the atheists and agnostics of Faith World—created their own group more for camaraderie rather than to have an Order.

On a large vid-screen, Archbishop Masai speaks to them from Africa.

"Our African Catholic Council had a lengthy meeting with Prophet Simon of the Mormon Order and his Apostles. It was then we learned what really happened in Russia to instigate their Purge with all their religious citizens being removed from Greater Russia into Europa. The Russians are especially adept at media blackouts. We know that the previous Russian president died—I use that word reservedly—but the succeeding president, this gangster, survived an assassination attempt...by the Pope Patriarch of the Russian Orthodox."

There are gasps in the meeting hall.

"I met the Pope Patriarch many times, though it has been several years since I last saw him. But the man I knew never would or could do any such thing, let alone leap out windows and climb buildings like a spider.

"We now have another piece of the puzzle in terms of what happened to the East Orthodox and Behemoth. If he went insane or was replaced somehow by some kind of doppelganger, then that's why none of us have been able to find them. Because it was not the Russians or any government. It was a conspiracy of one— the Pope Patriarch. God only knows what happened and we can only pray that the Russian Orthodox people did not suffer some deadly fate. We can only pray that we may see them safe again in the future."

"If he did go insane...if he was responsible, could he have seized Behemoth by himself, without his people?" one of the Continuum members asks.

Prophet Simon is on another vid-screen on the wall. "Sadly, the answer is yes. Behemoth is very much like Leviathan. We call it a 'living ship' because of its advanced AI offensive and defensive systems, but it is its DNA and brainwave interface with its pilots that makes such a thing possible. We have already built in safeguards because..." He pauses for a moment. Everyone in the room knows why and the Mormons will never speak of it. "We built in safeguards to make sure no one could use Leviathan against our people, including me, but the same safeguards were not implemented in Behemoth."

"Leviathan is water-based. Behemoth was land-based. My God, I hope he didn't do a mass-suicide somewhere," another Continuum member says.

"There is no way to know," Masai says, "but we all have surveillance drones searching."

"Archbishop, you said doppelganger. Do we now suspect that?" Rabbi Kanter of the Shamar Order asks.

"We already know from our own operatives and others that President T. Wilson's Project New People, and comparable programs in other countries by other governments and by other groups, included the ability to create biological sim-clones and bio-android copies. We haven't done anything with the information, other than for Mexico, but we're talking about at least three countries, and why not other leaders?" Masai asks rhetorically.

"There are also various 'Manchurian Candidate' programs in existence," Kanji of the Shogun Order adds. "Narco-psychological conditioning. We may never know what was done to the Pope Patriarch or if it was really him."

"That is why I sounded the alarm at New Lerdo Church during Pope Marco's Inauguration Ceremony. I heard about some sick man on his way to the Church. Prophet Simon told me about the Pope Patriarch situation, we all know about the rumors of Russian President Igor turning himself into a monster, the news that the Delivery Man with the Man Made Out of String disappearing again. For all I knew this man could have been the Delivery Man android. I couldn't take the chance."

"What happened to that man?" another Continuum member asks.

"He disappeared. There's no way he could have gotten away from us, but he did."

"But was there a plot?" another Continuum member asks. "We just got through talking about the Igor's bomb situation. We were all panicking that the Russian Bloc was trying to drop a fission bomb on Faithers when in fact it was a move against American, Caliphate, and CHIN enemy subs. The last time I saw panic in the enclaves like this was when we first built the enclaves and felt the government was going to come over the horizon any moment. It's so easy for people to believe the worst. My children were crying for days, scared that our own president would do the same here—drop bombs on us."

"And we take responsibility for that," Vincent of the Mormon Order says. "We should have gotten that information disseminated immediately."

"We all should have," Sister Serena of the Catholic Order says. "I'm so glad we have the Cowboy Rabbi creating this Cowboy Coalition because it seems that we can only contend with one crisis at a time. There we had two."

"What about the death, possible assassination, of the former Russian president that did happen? Who was responsible? All of those smiling pictures of him with the three superpowers: Peace in Our Time. We all knew something bad was going to come from their summit."

"The Lords of Earth, indeed. The Lords of Hell."

The Lords of Earth. The cutesy phrase coined by a reporter many years ago for the world's three superpowers. President of the United States Torrey E.C. Wilson has been in the White House for twenty-three years now, known by the public as President T. Wilson since he is the second president of America to have the last name. The Emperor Al-Siddiq has ruled the Supreme Islamic Caliphate for about the same length of time; during his reign, expanded their territorial conquests with the Fall of Jewish Israel, the destruction of Palestine Israel, and into Africa with the now-stalemated Islamic-Christian War. His late father led the Fall of Western Europe—all of Western Europe falling to radical Islam decades ago, with millions of people fleeing, those fortunate enough to escape. President Wen rules the other Pagan-majority empire, the Chinese-Indian Alliance, or CHIN. The previous reign of his father, which forced the union with India to create the Alliance, saw the decline of the Russian Bloc and the cessation of Caliphate incursions into CHIN territories.

"We will never know. With the exception of their current president, everyone who was physically there on site is now dead. All of us have theories, but they are only theories. And the Russian Bloc government doesn't seem to want to know either."

"We're calling these clones made to look like specific persons doppelgangers now?"

"It was never about what we call their Hitler Project. Creating clones of mass murderers—Hitler, Stalin, Mao, and others. Their Project New People was always about furthering their super-soldier programs."

"They were sim-clones—simulated clones, not actual clones, because there is no surviving DNA of the subjects. Be careful not to fall into the same science fiction fallacy traps that the public does," Kanji of the Shinto Order says. "They have gone past cloning to full biological manipulation, which cloning is only a small part of. They are so fixated on the ability to create biologicals that can effectively combat and destroy machines. They have merely figured out that they create doppelgangers for political purposes as an added benefit."

"How do we plan to counter this? We have already concluded Project Tek-Fall. Faithers don't do super soldiers or MMLs. We do robots and robot suits, androids, drones, mechanical weapons, energy weapons, even biological weapons, but not super soldiers or man-made life forms."

Wings of the Magi Order speaks. "Nor should we. The Magi Order will handle the issue of super soldiers. We have reversible bio-cybernetic tek that can deal with any human, humanoid, or animal threats created."

"You mean the demons."

"Yes, we've been dealing with them since the late '60s."

"What of this Keeper? She's the mother of these things, isn't she?"

"She's the mother of the American ones. But we destroyed them all. She's not the mother of the ones in other countries. The Internationalists are, but we successfully destroyed their main Zoo facility. And the Keeper destroyed all her potential successors, with our guidance. May I suggest we table this part of the discussion? It is something that shouldn't worry the Continuum."

"What does the Magi worry about?"

"The security, longevity, and prosperity of Faith World. The same as everyone else in the Continuum."

Moses and M notice Sek standing next to the open area of the Coliseum seats. He makes eye contact with them, holds up two fingers, and types the air. Moses looks at his tablet, M leans in also, and they read the message.

Tova of the Conservative Jewish Order is the only one standing from her seat, reading from her table-top tablet. "For our Brazil op, we'd like to praise the new Continuum Medical Corps under the leadership of Rabba Silva. The highest praise from the Sisters Guerras, who we all know don't compliment easily, for the fine work of our Amish, Mennonite, Orthodox, and Hasidic medics in attending to the more than six thousand women in distress that were rescued."

The Continuum audience give loud applause from their seats.

"Also praise for Sister Serena and the Sisters Guerras for bringing an end to the Slave Wars in Brazil. The 'good guys' did the winning. We now have firm bases of operations in the Spanish Americas to effectively move to the eradication of all slavery in the remaining thirty percent of the Spanish Americas. With Mexico, Central America, and now Brazil gone to them, their days are numbered."

Applause again.

"We praise in advance the Hasidim who will be creating a new Dog Corps for the Continuum for small, highly specialized operations where biologic rather than technological detection methods are required."

Applause.

"And we praise in advance the work of Yohan, the Cowboy Rabbi, in creating another much needed, already mentioned, force for the Continuum. An advance, paramilitary force for medium to large operations. That of the Cowboy Coalition."

Applause.

"We praise Elliott Finegold in taking the lead in the highly-controversial One Project for both the Jewish and Protestant Orders, in seeing our remaining Hidden and Lot Faithers around the world rejoin with our enclaves.

"And to settle the question of the Jewish and Christian Exiles, Mr. Elliott has already enlisted the Gnostics and the Shinto Order in his task. I don't envy him—none of us do—but we all know that if there is a person who can see us through this to the end, it is Elliott. Thank you for leading this."

Applause again.

Another face appears on one of the vid-screens.

"And finally, we formally acknowledge the new Pope of the Catholic Order, Pope Marcos I."

All the seated Continuum members rise to their feet to give standing applause.

8:02 p.m., 10 October 2096

Dinner was light, and afterward the Continuum senior leaders convene in a small conference room. After the full Continuum meeting, such smaller follow-up and planning meetings happen well into the night.

All the attendees are of the Protestant Order—the merging of all the collapsing denominations of the past in the latter 2080s—Anglican, Baptist, Church of God in Christ, Episcopalian, Lutheran, Methodist, Pentecostal, Presbyterian, Southern Baptist, and others, including American Catholics who decided to convert. The only non-Protestants are the Catholics, Niccolo and Augustín, and the Conservative Jews, Tova, and Mr. Tova.

Augustín shakes his head at hearing the explanation from M.

"That was the Finger of God Project. That's…ruthless."

Dale, one of the Protestant leaders, responds, "They had their blasphemous 'Good Bible' and mandatory Registration Initiatives, their Project Purity, their great grand ghetto concentration camp in the center of the country. Sending their registration compliance officers into our churches and synagogues. It was bad. It was civil war."

Augustín holds up his arm to calm him. "I'm Mexican. You had to deal with anti-religious governments. So did we in our country. We began our fight a century and a half earlier and have been dealing with our own anti-religious, Plutarco Calles-style governments ever since *and* criminal narco-cartels." He smiles.

"We *like* ruthless." He glances at Niccolo. "You were right."

"I told you," Niccolo says. "Faithers in America are not the Faithers in America of the past. They not only caught up to us in the ruthless area, I think they've surpassed us."

"High praise coming from a Sicilian." Dale manages a laugh.

"A very provocative operation," Augustín says.

"It was a very provocative op," Tova adds, "but we all approved it."

"However, I will confess that such an op would probably not have been approved today," Moses says. "They have their hands full with Anarchists, so we stay away. Out of sight, out of mind. Let them attack and kill each other."

"Is it another op of ours?" Augustín asks.

"Mr. Augustín, we would never incite distrust and violence among our anti-Faither atheist brethren in Tek World. We would never do that."

Augustín smirks at his sarcasm.

"There's no possible way they could know about the Finger of God Project," Bishop Cyrus says. He maintains his clerical title despite the fact that his old Order merged into the new Protestant Order.

"Red Hat is dead," Moses says again.

"It doesn't mean anything," Mr. Tova says. "He wasn't even a Faither. For all we know, he was mugged or surprised a burglar. Those crimes do still happen, even in the tek-cities."

"Moses, I know that look. This is not the days in the height of the Resistance. We're not the street revolutionaries we once were. We're heads of state now. We're not an underground movement. We have our own independent cities. We cannot do anything provocative. We're in the middle of Project Noah," Thaddeus says. "We all know the stakes."

"There's nothing that suggests a sanctioned government hit. Nothing," Cyrus adds.

"I don't believe in coincidences," Moses says.

"But they do legitimately happen," Cyrus counters.

"I agree with Moses," Niccolo says. "I don't believe in coincidences either."

"But what do we have? Nothing."

"One." Niccolo holds up his hand with one finger. "One of your deep operatives gets himself killed."

"The op was seven years ago. Why now?" another leader asks.

"Two. Some strange man shows up in New Lerdo City the very day of the Pope's inauguration ceremony and vanishes. No one can find him. His image is not even on any sat-recon. None of our street intel saw where he went."

"But nothing happened. You said he didn't even get close to Pope Marcos," a female leader says.

"Three," Niccolo continues, "the Mexican Parliament had convened secretly for some unknown purpose."

"For what purpose?" M asks.

"I believe it was to get ready for an imminent attack on the Pope. Spin the news somehow for their own political agenda," Augustín answers.

"What agenda?" M asks.

"I don't know. I'm not an anti-Faither atheist. Something nefarious. I can run down the list of everything they want to do."

M gestures with her hands. "I have to agree with the side of restraint. We did table the discussion to the next full meeting. What about the Bull?" she looks at Niccolo.

"We have everything in place. He won't win his re-election."

"Then our person wins."

"Yes."

"So that takes care of your main political threat. Do you have anything that points to a deliberate effort to escape from your forces, this sick man? Niccolo, be objective. Not your instincts, or gut, or third eye. We Faithers are the most paranoid living things on the planet, but couldn't this man have stumbled away? Is it possible?"

"It's possible."

"What about the other two? The Lion and the Turtle?" Augustín asks.

The Bull was the nickname for the current Mexican president, a gregarious man in the public eye, but when the vid-cams weren't recording was a spiteful, morose man given to violent tirades and political retributions. Miles Whitehall was the Prime Minster of Canada. He has flowing white hair to match his sideburns and beard. His nickname is the White Lion in political circles. The brash Joaquim Jimenas is one of the youngest men ever elected as President of Brazil. He is known for his strange fascination with turtles; the grounds of his private mansion housed some sixteen different rare species and he even named his children after different turtles.

"I'm still not convinced that they are doppelgangers, to use the term we've been using," Cyrus says. "Though, the information from the Mormons does support the theory and that this is a global threat."

"May I ask, who cares?" Dale interjects. "Clones, android-copies, whatever, let them create their own Five Cities. We don't live in it. We'll respond to any threats as we always do, whether real human or doppelganger or anything else. Does it matter?"

"It matters," Niccolo answers. "We may not live in their tek-cities, but we still live on this planet. Mexico, Canada, and Brazil. Possibly the same happened in Russia. It matters. We must always know the what, how, and why of what our enemies do. Always—that is our mission as leaders, of all of us in the Continuum."

"Obviously, I agree, but I don't want us to ever think we can save the world. We can't, nor should that be even an indirect mission. We can do a lot of good in the world, but we can't make the world good."

"Sek, do we have anything at all that points to some Grid government plot against Red Hat? Anything?" M asks.

Sek pauses. "No."

"Let's be clear," M adds. "If we ever get that proof, I'll be the first to second the motion for retaliation. But we need to continue our withdrawal from them, not reintroduce ourselves to them. And speaking of paranoid. They are so focused on the Anarchists and others in the Trog-land territories."

"Exactly. When your two enemies are trying to kill each other, you don't jump in between them," Sapphire, another leader, says.

Moses just looks off into space, thinking.

"Moses, will you let this go? We know that look," Cyrus asks.

"Moses?" his wife M asks.

"Who do we have with the most recent experience working in Homeland?" Moses asks.

The group thinks for a moment.

"One of our members was actually an agent out of their Florida Regional Office," Tova answers. She smiles. "They never once suspected him until he left."

"Did we ever meet him?"

"I'm not sure. It was Gideon."

"He retired, though."

"Yes. More like an extended sabbatical. Why do you want to talk with him?"

"I appreciate that you all do not want us to respond with any evidence," Moses says. "But in my mind, we have to find that evidence. If these three separate incidents were a deliberate, secret plot against us, then we have to know, because it means our enemies have vastly improved their effectiveness. We have to know for certain. It's better to be over-cautious than not cautious enough."

"You really think there is a conspiracy?" Thaddeus asks.

"There's always a conspiracy. We know about all the others. Let's make sure this isn't a new one we don't know about."

"We have to be very careful," Dalmatia, another leader, adds. "We mustn't do anything to jeopardize the Project, especially after losing all of Behemoth. We're so close. We can't afford to go to war with the government again."

"That's precisely why I don't believe it's a coincidence. And we're forgetting the claims of these Exiles. How did they know about the Catholic's ceremony?"

"But they told us about it, and if something had happened, then we would have known for sure," Tova says.

"It's okay to live with a heart that sees the glass as half full, but the head must always see it as half empty," Niccolo says. "We went through this in the Middle East. We survived, but many did not. I agree with Moses. We must know, not wish it away and hope for the best or 'leave it to God.' That's Muslim talk. People have a strange habit of attributing much of what is their responsibility to God. We're the leaders. Followers have the luxury to blindly be optimistic. We do not."

"The Exiles telling us would notify us. That's not a very good way to conduct a plot," Cyrus says.

"Galerius and company are not the grand spy masters they think themselves to be. They slip up all the time," Dale adds.

"If they hit us in Mexico, one of our foundational members,

and succeeded, what do you think would have been the impact to the Continuum? It would have been catastrophic, in every sense. It would be the equivalent of them hitting us here and now at a full Continuum Meeting. We can be cautious, but the question must be answered for the Continuum," Moses says. "Are we under attack?"

M asks Sek, "Where do you stand?"

"I have no opinion. Some of you feel there is a threat. Some of you want to be cautious because of The Project, which is of singular importance. For me the matter is simple—elevate the threat level. In fact, I've already done so. I've activated all Templar reserves for additional security and surveillance. I don't need a majority or even any facts. All I need is one of you with a suspicion. You're the generals; I'm the generals' bodyguard. My job is very straightforward and no different than my colleague counterparts in the other Orders."

"Mr. Blond would do the same in Mexico and the Four Brothers in Africa," Niccolo says. "And we all know Shoshana's M.O."

Sek continues, "Your job is more complicated. But if this is a new pure conspiracy plot, the Project must take second chair. Otherwise, we could lose everything. The risk is worth it, even if it delays the Project."

"What do you hope to accomplish with Gideon then?" Mr. Tova asks Moses.

"Understand the Grid government's latest protocols to a granular level. If there is a conspiracy, then there's a file. If there is a file, then we have the best teks on the planet to steal that file. And if there is a file to be stolen and we do and it says what we suspect, then our retaliation should be nothing short of hellish."

Lords of Babylon

**The Gideon Residence, Gamaliel Enclave, Florida
Panhandle Wastelands
8:56 a.m., 14 October 2096**

A slight breeze moves across the surface of the Olympic-sized pool that usually is in use at this time of day. But no swimming laps this morning, Gideon relaxes in his pod-chair in his flowery top and black shorts as the music plays softly and a fan blows from the chair nozzles. Staring at the pool and the sky, he drinks his morning coffee. The entire backyard, with the house ten yards behind him, is a plush green lawn surrounded by a white picket fence.

He is in quiet, content contemplation.

**The Wall, Gamaliel Enclave, Florida Panhandle Wastelands
9:22 a.m., 14 October 2096**

Auto-drive takes their two-seater car to the main gate and a robot eye—a bulb-like device on a wire-like arm—peers into the car and then scans the men from head to toe. Other robot eyes scan the entire car—top, bottom, inside and outside.

Two men are inside. NIS (his nickname, "Notoriously Invasive Species") is a slim, dark-skinned man with unusual circular eyeglasses that glow an intermittent neon blue. He was formerly of the Catholic Order, specifically the African Collective, but converted to Protestantism when he returned to America. Goli is a giant of a man, seven feet tall and all muscles. His parents were of the Israeli Jewish Order, but ever since he was thirteen years old, he has been a member of the Conservative Jewish Order. The men are the top tek-lords of the entire Continuum—teks so brilliant that their skills are viewed as inexplicable, even impressing the Magi Order on occasion.

"Please state your name, receiver, and code," the robot says to him.

"Goli. We're here to see Gideon. 64572. We're expected."

"Confirmed. Proceed inside."

The gate opens. Over the archway, in Hebrew, are the words:

"I DO NOT WANT FOLLOWERS WHO ARE RIGHTEOUS, RATHER I WANT FOLLOWERS WHO ARE TOO BUSY DOING GOOD THAT THEY WON'T HAVE TIME TO DO BAD." – THE KOTZKER REBBE (1787–1859)

The two men park their vehicle first and are shuttled through the residential streets by an enclave driverless pod car. Quaint neutral-colored homes with children playing in their yards or in the street (kickball or laser-stick ball are the favorites), adults relaxing on their porches, mowing lawns or tending their gardens, sitting and conversing on yard furniture, lounging by or swimming in the pool.

The doorbell is still echoing through the house when a shapely redhead holding a toddler answers her door.

"Hello, Goli," she says.

"Hello, Natasha." He plants a kiss on her check.

"Goli, I hope you're not still growing. You always seem taller when I see you." She turns to the other man. "You must be Mr. NIS."

"Nice to meet you." NIS removes his dark-tinted circular spectacles and shakes her free hand. "How are you, little one?" He shakes the little boy's hand, who starts to giggle.

"He's in the back." She points with her chin.

The walls in the house are filled with family photos of both Gideon and Natasha's families—an entire family tree. Some of the photos go back centuries, as evidenced by old black-and-white pictures. They exit the rear patio door through the wind-wall—blowing to keep out any flying insects—and they see him. His back is to them. Immediately a mischievous expression comes over Goli's face and he begins to crouch down.

"Don't even try it, Goli," Gideon calls out. "Giants are not very good at sneaking up on people and I'm already watching you on my armrest monitor."

"Gideon, you're no fun," Goli answers back.

Gideon sets down his coffee to stand and face his visitors. The two men embrace with bear hugs. NIS extends a hand, but Gideon gives him a hug too.

"This is a hugging household," he says.

Gideon reaches down to his pod-chair and touches a few buttons and the men can see two other pod-chairs, hovering in the air, coming to them.

"Touch them and place where you want," Gideon says.

"Looks like the retired husband and father life is treating you well," Goli notes.

With the auto-hovering, the pod-chairs seem weightless as Goli and NIS set them next to Gideon's on either side.

"It is."

"You're too young to retire," NIS says.

Gideon sits back down, and they do the same.

"I resigned," Gideon says.

"Resigning your commission as a leader in the Continuum," NIS says. "Someone at your level. That's unusual for this critical time."

"Time is always critical." Gideon picks up his coffee. "I had an epiphany back on one of my many missions. I was naked, cold, running barefoot through the streets of some Godless tek-city. I said to myself, I have no wife, no kids. Here I am being hunted by shadow drones. If I die, what would I leave behind? It's one thing for Jesus to be a thirty-year-old Jew with no wife and kids, but not me."

"I completely understand," NIS says.

"'Good things come to those who wait is a universal adage," Gideon says. "But so is, 'there is no such thing as tomorrow.'"

NIS smiles. "I hear you."

He looks at Goli. "So how's married life for you?"

"What's the word I'm looking for?" Goli thinks. "*Shocking*. But I'll say good."

The men laugh.

"I have never, ever heard someone describe their marriage like that."

"I'm married to the leader of the Jewish Wolf-Pack. You should have committed me to a mental institution. That's what best men are supposed to do."

"I wasn't about to get into the middle of that. I told you that once she set her sights on you that your fate was sealed."

"I thought you were being philosophical, not literal."

"Kids?"

"First one on the way," Goli says with a smile.

"So what can this retired spy do for you two?"

"We need you for validation purposes," NIS answers.

"Validation? What does that mean?"

"We want to pick your brain for a bit," Goli says.

"What exactly?" Gideon asks.

"Babylon," NIS answers.

"The Pagans' VR world?"

"The largest in the world."

"How does that help you? And I don't think I've ever played a vid-game in my life."

"Babylon is part of the Grid."

"I see where you're going, but they're separate. Government infrastructure services, the energy grid, surveillance grid, financial grid, registry, data collection. They're all firewalled. Lots of people have come up with the same idea, though I'm not sure about using a VR world to breach into the Grid. Homeland heavily monitors VR worlds."

"True," Goli says.

"And Goli, you're on Homeland's top ten most wanted listed in the cyber-terrorism division. Don't you have to be more careful than that? They've got tek-lords too—cyber bounty hunters."

"I know. Three of the top ten tek-lords in the world are government cyber-trackers."

"And I suppose you two are part of the top ten?"

"That wounds me, Gideon. I thought we were friends."

"Okay, okay, top ten tek-lord member. I don't know what I can tell you. I never worked for the cyber division. You know that. Field agent my entire time in Homeland."

"You know more than you think you know."

"If you say."

Goli takes a collapsible tablet from his sleeve pouch. He extends it and the device turns on automatically. "We want you to look at a personnel directory. Touch the images of anyone you recognize by sight or by name, even if you never personally met them."

"And?"

"We'll do the rest."

"How long is this going to take?"

"An hour or two. Depends how fast your fingers work."

"Goli, I'm supposed to be retired." He takes the tablet from Goli and begins touching faces on the screen. "What is this going to allow you two to do? You can't breach the American Grid through a VR world. It's a virtual cesspool of vid-game addicts, VR world addicts, VR sex game addicts—every kind of degenerate you can imagine is in there, but the firewalls there are the same as if it were the White House mainframe."

"So if someone could breach Babylon, they could breach the White House or any other government system?"

Gideon looks up. "What are you not telling me?"

"Nothing at all." NIS just smiles.

"I know you're not telling me everything. I can tell. Goli is always quiet when he's plotting something. He's been like that since we were kids."

"No plotting. Just two tek-heads doing their necessary external research. Don't overthink things, Gideon," Goli says. "Do you want to be here an hour or two, or three hours, or four?"

"Oh, it's like that." Gideon continues scrolling through the profiles. "Whatever you two are going to do, I don't want anything to tie back to me. I'm out of it and I'm staying out."

"Yes, Family Man Gideon," Goli mocks.

"You're right behind me, Family Man Goli. Goli was trouble enough by himself. Now you have a wingman." Goli and NIS start laughing. "I shudder to think what's going to be happening in the world now."

"There's three of us actually," NIS adds.

"Oh, God help us. Three of you. Just keep all your tek-madness away from me."

The Room, Unknown Location
6:45 a.m., 16 October 2096

In the beginning, analogy was first, then digital, then technology, and now tek. The world is so dependent on technology that those who can create and maintain it are the true gods of society. Those who can hack into it and take possession are part genius, part artist, and all criminal. Governments hunt these 'tek-lords.' They are perpetual threats to Tek World. The best ones, the legendary ones, are all Faithers.

A large cavernous room is filled with rows and rows of half-circle cubicles. Teks are hard at work typing, scrolling, and using stylus pens on their systems. No one has less than three vid-screens on their desk, some have as many as seven. Everyone is wearing dark glasses that allow them to view multiple pop-up virtual displays. No one is talking in the room. There's too much work to do.

A young Asian woman sits in a large spherical lobby wearing a simple cream colored suit (chao fu). She is the only person waiting. She looks up, wondering how many human and mechanical eyes are watching her.

An entrance appears on the wall opposite her and a lanky man runs out.

"Sorry to keep you waiting, Ms. Zen."

She stands. "It's quite all right."

He shakes her hand. "I've always wanted to meet you."

"Really? Why is that?"

"You knocked down Father Marcos' world record in *Kill the Devil*. Well, he's the Catholic's Pope now."

The vid-game Kill the Devil, still quite popular in Faith World, has the player go through different levels of Hell to kill its cartoon devil any way you can with gunfire, knives, body blows, etc., while he tries a variety of ways to maim or kill you in violent or disgusting ways.

"It's not too impressive to beat someone in a vid-game and he set his record over five years ago. He doesn't play anymore, and if he did, he'd probably still be fighting for the top. But life takes precedence over vid-games."

"But you have the records in Armageddon, Tribulation, and End Times."

"You really do follow me."

He leads her through Skeleton Pass, the name for the connecting hallway to the Room. It glows with a light that has a very strange blue quality. They are no longer human beings, but walking skeletons with translucent skins. Any cybernetic implants, and even any synthetically grown organs or limbs, will register.

"Are you of the Shinto Order or…"

"I'm not religious if that's what you're asking."

"Oh. A Gnostic?"

"I'm not affiliated with the Gnostics. I'm of the Shinto Order."

"As a…"

"As a Pagan, yes. Though that is an American term. Outside of America we say atheist."

"An atheist in a Christian Order. That seems…illogical."

She grins. "God doesn't need me to believe in Her."

The man chuckles.

"I didn't offend you with my pronoun, did I?" she asks.

"Of course not. Pronouns are a human creation. He's not any gender, so no pronoun is technically accurate, but the masculine is tradition. We like tradition."

"The existence of God is not a certainty for me. Isn't truthfulness a Faither principle?"

"It is."

"Then I'm being truthful. I don't believe in Him. I believe in His people. It has been over two thousand years since all of this happened. People can't get an event accurate that happened last week. Something happened, I'm sure of that, but what happened—I'm not positive about that."

"Interesting."

"And you?"

"The African Collective. Of the Armenian Christian Order."

"My reasons for living with the Shogun on Shinto Island and being part of the leadership is very logical. They're going to Heaven and Neo-Japan and the rest of Asia is going to Hell."

"You believe in Heaven and Hell?"

"I do. And here on Earth, a final comeuppance to a people— the good and the bad."

"Interesting. I never heard that reasoning before."

"Because you never met me before."

Finally they walked through a cloud of mist, which renders any bio-, micro- or nano-tek inoperable. No external tek or devices are allowed in or out. They are no longer skeletons as they pass through the final nano-door into the Room. None of the teks look up from their screens as they walk past down an aisle. She is led to a mini-meeting room, where two men wait. Zen enthusiastically shakes Goli's hand as she bows and repeats the same with NIS.

"It is an honor to meet you, Goli-san. It is an honor to meet you, NIS-san." She reaches into her breast jacket pocket. "I wish to give you these as a gift from me and the teks of the Shinto Order who did not have the privilege and honor of meeting you."

"We are just men," Goli says. "Nothing special."

"Honorable men always say that. Kanji, our leader, is the same way. But as a fellow tek-lord, we know you both are much more than that. I have studied your methods in every detail. Goli-san, your attack methods are materializing into systems—as if burrowing in somehow, microscopically or possibly atomically, through unexpected vulnerabilities that no one would readily imagine—and then overwhelm, consume, expand to destroy every part of it. NIS-san, your attack method is flow into a system using its own inherent properties and then use electrical or quasi-electrical means to destroy. There is a list of the top ten tek-lords in the world. Does this mean I am part of this list now?"

"Not yet," Goli answers. "You're in the next tier of ten, but after this op, you will be among the ten."

"That suggests that someone on the list will no longer be there. Not because of my tek-abilities."

"Zen, your tek-abilities are irrelevant. You are here because of your knowledge."

"Knowledge?"

"Vid-games," NIS says.

Zen's face saddens. "I've been invited here because I play vid-games. NIS-san, you play vid-games, but you are much more than that. I am much more too."

Goli says, "We understand that you secretly play in Babylon. The last ten years or so?"

Unknown Transport Site, Trog-land
12 Midnight, 17 October 2096

When the hover jet arrived, the three tek-lords boarded. They sit together as the only passengers.

"What is this Finger of God?" asks Zen.

"It was an op done during the time we still called ourselves the Resistance," Goli answers.

"We're still the Resistance."

"We're the Continuum now. It was directed at T. Wilson himself."

"Was that wise?"

"He would never have known what was done to him, but would have known it was us. The details are not important. It was seven years ago and truthfully we don't care either way. Our enemies don't define the Continuum anymore."

"Yes, we transcend them," Zen adds. "I heard the General Moses speech."

"Yes."

"We're about to engage in some pre-transcendental violence?"

"Yes."

Zen smiles at them from her seat facing them. "Good. One can't stare at rock gardens and meditate all the time."

Babylon, the Net
Time: Unclear

Freespace—a region of the Net that is not run or sponsored by a government; free of any government monitoring or tracing. But Freespace is also infested with cyber-pirates, who attempt to seize control of your link for their own purposes or follow it back to you, where they can do such wonderful things as steal your identity or hack into your systems; dark worms, that eat any data you capture from the Net; and freddies that corrupt any data you download from the Net. These are just the main Net predators; there are dozens of other types. It is very much like maneuvering through a jungle teeming with ferocious wild animals.

But it is also where Babylon reigns, and thousands of other virtual reality worlds exist.

A man walks into the pulsating pink R and R pleasure bar through a hallway shrouded in clouds of multi-colored vapor. A busty woman in a virtually see-through dress and a topless man wearing translucent pants greet him at the entrance.

All throughout the establishment are attractive women and men clustered together in groups at the bar, at individual tables, and in the shadows at the back of the place on the way to the restrooms.

"Male or female?" the man asks.

"Female," Tapeworm answers.

"Homo or hetero?" the woman asks.

"Bi or tri?" the man asks.

"Hetero and let's see where the day takes us."

All the men in the R and R bar disappear and music starts playing. The strobe lights spin as women seem to appear out of nowhere to take to the dance floor—some dancing as couples, others dancing with everyone around them.

Tapeworm sits in one of the booths, as a woman on each side of him hold the top of his head with sucker-tipped fingers. His eyes flutter, alternating with different rainbow colors—his mind in an almost dream-like state as the hallucinogenic stream pulses through his brain.

A bean-pole woman in a very tiny sleeveless, one-piece dress glides across the floor.

"You have clients waiting, but work is forbidden in Babylon."

"My clients have to play too or I don't work for them."

"Very smart. They said they'd meet you outside when you're done." She smiles and glides away.

"Then it will be a long wait."

Tapeworm exits the R and R pleasure bar. It looks like any tek-city but the buildings are alternating colors of pink, orange, lavender, powder blue, and many more. This chromatic flux is in all things in Babylon—the clouds, the cars, people's clothes and hair color are constantly changing. People don't walk; they glide, hovering above the ground, to where they wish to go or simply teleport there.

He sees his clients—two men waiting. One of them is a tall giant of a man, all muscles. Must be a pudgy midget in the real world, he thinks to himself. The other is a tan-skinned man with neon-blue, circular lens glasses—one can almost make out the constant static charges from them. While everyone in Babylon dresses in the boldest and brightest colors and in the most provocative outfits, the giant is dressed in a black office suit with white shirt and black tie; the other man in a blue office suit with white shirt and blue tie.

Who wears office suits in Babylon? Obviously VR virgins, Tapeworm says to himself.

A male-female couple is walking down the yellow-brick road encircling the pleasure bar, hand-in-hand, when they are both harpooned. Giant spears penetrate their bodies, hooks spread out, and they are yanked up into the air. The flying pirate ship descends from the sky and everyone on the streets scatter for safety—all except him—and the two men waiting for him.

The cyber-pirate ship pulls up their two victims and jets off as walking cannons appear and start firing lasers at them, but too late. The cyber-pirate ship phases out of Babylon.

Tapeworm looks back at NIS and Goli with a smirk. The men teleported right next to him. "It's a terrible thing to have your entire Net-identity stolen like that," he says to them. "Got to be careful in Babylon."

"Yes, you must." Tapeworm sees the men's mouths move in unison, but the voice was female and didn't seem to come from their mouths.

"We're the only three on this city block who didn't lose our heads—or our bodies," he says. "One would have to be some kind of tek-lord not to be afraid of a fortified cyber-pirate ship."

"We would indeed," the big man says.

"But there are only two of you."

"No, there are three of us. Just like there are three of you," glasses man says.

"Your one person is watching my two comrades."

"Yep," glasses man says.

"Who are you? You obviously know me."

"I'm Goli."

"I'm NIS."

"How confrontational. My 'clients' are quite sneaky."

"We've been looking for you."

"Why is that?"

"We need a data download."

"Why tell me?"

"True. You will only deny us, so we'll have to take it instead."

"What's to stop me from exiting this instant?"

"You'd never live that down. A couple of Jew-Christian fugitive tek-lords scaring away the legendary Tapeworm."

"Trying to play my ego against me, but in Babylon I am invincible, and my comrades too."

"Are you now?"

"Yes. We are the Lords of Babylon."

"We thought that's what we are."

"You're not, because we can do anything here." Tapeworm's skin starts to bubble.

"But we know how to maneuver around all the venal badness," Goli says.

"And we wear clean clothes to keep all the fleas off of us," NIS adds.

"Those must be very clean clothes to keep fleas off of you."

"How did you know it was me, the great Tapeworm? My way with the ladies, was it?"

"It's written on your belt."

Tapeworm looks down to see the words on his black belt.

"You write so much code trying to be clever that you forgot what you already wrote in earlier scenarios."

"I don't see any words on your bodies, so I don't believe you are who you say you are."

"We thought our gadgets would give us away. We do have a notorious reputation."

Tapeworm's eyes narrow. "NIS and Goli. Goli and NIS. Who's the third?"

"Why should we tell you? You're figuring it all out."

"Zen. It must be Zen."

"You've tried to kill or capture us all these years. Now we're right here in front of you," Goli says. "I'm going to beat the wall with your body."

"Ha ha. Do you think you know where I am? Government tek-hunters are housed in deep underground bunkers when on assignment. You think we'd be stupid to work anywhere else. No Jew-Christian, we are as secure as the president. Try another Jedi mind-trick because that one goes nowhere. Do you think you're the first to think of that?

"Wall. Body." Goli points at him. "Smash!"

"We're speaking in baby syllables now. So it's Jew-Christians who evolved from monkeys. You made a big mistake, Jew-Christians. You won't escape me and your comrade won't escape us. Yes, I've been hunting you a long time, but it comes to an end now. Thanks to you. We'd decompile all of Babylon to get you two."

Tapeworm acts as if he's going to say more, but lunges at them—his arms become giant worm-like tentacles with teethed sucker ends as he violently penetrates their chests. NIS and Goli's holo-identities go out of phase as their bodies shake.

NIS's glasses come back into phase and blasts him with laser beams, ripping Tapeworm's arms off as the rest of his body is propelled backwards. Tapeworm lands on the street as he watches Goli's body begin to grow to nine feet in height in seconds; his hands become cupped slings as he continues to grow and expand to grab a nearby pod-car.

Tapeworm's legs become worm-like, entwine and burrow into the ground, pulling himself underground just as the pod-car crashes where he was.

Surge has Zen wrapped in his tentacle arms and his entire body gyrates with glowing, vibrating electric pulses burning Zen's holo-identity. The other tek-lord assassin, Malaria, stands nearby laughing at her screams and then de-materializes his body into a million pieces of floating black dust.

NIS and Goli stand on the street as they watch Zen fly to them on giant, translucent butterfly wings.

"We don't have time for this," she says. "I don't want to play vid-games. We can't kill them. We can only disrupt them. This is never-ending."

NIS and Goli both notice it. A holo-identity of one of the many trapped people in Babylon is of a different resolution than anyone else's. Outwardly he is a plain man, dressed in a stringy purple suit with a fashionably ripped up white shirt and a black hat tilted down to conceal his face. He realizes they are watching him and he vanishes.

"Be patient," Goli says to Zen. "Learn from your elders."

"My elders? What's the plan, 'my elders'? They're government, so all they have to do is reset Babylon. They have that ability too. We can't do that. Look."

They turn to see the sky darkening with storm clouds.

NIS leans forward as a pen appears in his hand. He scribbles something on the palm of her hand and then turns to look back at the storm. Goli's holo-identity is growing in size again as NIS's blue-tinted glasses explode with discharges of red electricity.

Zen looks at her hand: THE GOAL IS NOT TO WIN. IT IS TO PLAY FOREVER!

Residential Quarter, Washington, DC
11:25 a.m., 19 October 2096

The director steps from his chauffeured car with a suitcase in each hand, and closes the door. As the car drives off, he takes in the sight. There is nothing like the City. Technology and urban construction so intertwined that it is so far beyond the definition of "city." And this tek-city metropolis is even more.

In the typical tek-city, none of the uncomfortable qualities of a season can ever fully impact the population—harsh cold, burning heat, and high winds are all kept at bay. Massive air-regulator machines are constructed right into almost every building and are centrally coordinated to either heat or cool the entire tek-city using advanced air-flow dynamics. Only heavy rains are allowed to invade, but that is more for urban management reasons. Let's give the city a quick shower. Solar and wind power still account for only the tiniest fraction of urban power consumption, as the Grid sucks such unimaginable amounts of energy by the nano-second. Primary energy is all fission, since nothing else can match the insatiable public demand.

The ever-flashing, ever-changing digital billboards on top of every commercial building lining either side of the street catch his attention next. Music, movies, clothes, the latest devices, latest cars, restaurants, vacation trips, virtual reality dens, drug parlors, massage services—the advertisements are everywhere. These advids are either rapid stop-motion live-def static photos or full-fledged vids. The colors are as bold and vibrant as the sounds are loud and frenetic. Both rapidly pulsate to create an atmosphere that completely engulfs the sight and hearing of anyone within range.

Above the buildings, a drone flies by. The sky is dotted with them, even more so than other cities. It's a globe surveillance model, a twenty-inch-diameter flying sphere in a muted silver color. Law enforcement use the drones to keep an ever-watchful vigil on the tek-city. In the past, these sophisticated flying vid-cams were twice their current size and more plane-shaped with short wings, but hover-tek has advanced so much, they can zip around more than a hundred feet in the air. People see them flying or hovering about so often that they forget about them, making the drones invisible in plain sight. With drones and Eyes—the common term for the government's ever-watching, ever-recording stationary vid-surveillance camera network—literally everywhere, the government monitors the tek-cities to instantly alert ground police of any disturbance, crime, or act of terrorism.

Additionally, Eyes are everywhere—the tek-city's stationary vid-cam surveillance system. But both drones and Eyes are far more than simple vid-surveillance. Mind-reading tek to read your emotional state, facial expressions, body language, perspiration rate. The audio not only analyzes voice intonations for signs of aggression or violence, but also reads your heart rate for elevated rates, indicating extreme nervousness—hello suicide bomber.

The streets are packed and brimming with life, energy, and excitement. There is nothing like the hustle and bustle of a tek-city, both the automation and the people. For tek-city dwellers, the styles of dress are endless. On one end of the scale, there are the traditional business types in their office suits, shirts, maybe vests, maybe ties, maybe not, in a variety of colors from simple blacks and whites to earth tones to natural rainbow colors to synthetic, techno colors, or even the so-called futuristic shiny silver everything, then the traditional faux-leather, plastic, cloth, or hemp dress shoes or the trendy glow boots or shoes.

Devices are carried by everyone—e-pads, each around the size of a large playing card; or the larger tablets, usually eight-by-eleven inches, with a handle or case. There are collapsible e-pads and tablets, and even wearable tek, the merging of device and clothing. Most of the people wear clear glasses, glowing with some type of light. No one has bad eyesight in this time; those who need corrective eye surgery receive it during the neonatal or natal stage. People wear clear glasses to attach their ear-sets, to avoid the in-ear versions or to use visual optical interface—text floating at the sides of your field of view—the current time, the name of a caller, the number of voice messages or emails, a dot indicating breaking news stories, etcetera—it can be programmed to display anything.

Despite the loud advids from the digital billboards, almost everyone in the streets are actively engaged in conversations on their devices of choice through ear-sets, a combination of phone, headset and ear bud, worn in one ear or both ears or attached to a pair of glasses so one can answer an incoming call, make a call, or voice interface—all these people talking aloud just adds to the daily urban craziness.

He can see the Capitol Dome and the Washington Monument looming in the distance. This is the nation's capitol and Pagans truly worship this town. And so does he.

Executive Branch, Non-Public Off-Site Offices, Washington, DC
11:35 a.m., 19 October 2096

There are forty thousand cities in America, but there is only one Washington, DC—the District, the tek-city above all others. The new director's first day on the job—so new that his office is not even ready.

The director waits at the entrance as an older man, in a similar dark office suit, meets him.

"Director," he greets.

"Good afternoon. I've only been in the job five minutes."

"How are you settling in?"

"I was a staffer here about two decades ago. The District hasn't changed at all. Wanted to see what life was like outside the Capitol. I did, so I'm back."

"It will be as if you never left. You'll be a good director for us."

He laughs. "Wait until you find out what kind of boss I am before the brown-nosing starts. I haven't even had my honeymoon period."

"Didn't they tell you?"

"Tell me?"

Secure Conference Room
Noon, 19 October 2096

Black-suited staffers are huddled around the vid-screens, grinning. "We have three tek-lord fugitives versus three tek-lord bounty hunters. Tell everyone! Start placing your bets!" one of the deputies says. "Let's get the pot as big as possible."

"How long have they been fighting?"

"Twenty-seven hours straight. I don't know how that's even possible."

"Oh, you're not a vid-game player are you? Your pod chair is the toilet and you have all your food in the chair for robot arms to feed you, and the real hardcore gamers feed intravenously. I've seen people plug in for months straight."

They hear a knock on the door and an agent pops his head in to signal them. He disappears back out and the men check their suits. The director enters and the men are almost at attention.

"Men."

"Director," they say.

"What do we have?"

He walks to their clustered vid-screens, looks at the displays, and then back up at them.

"What is going on with the Grid? What's causing the fluctuations?"

"It's Babylon, sir. There's some kind of event happening in there. It's leeching integrity strength from everywhere."

"How is a VR world doing that?" the director asks. "The Grid has primacy so how are they superseding that?"

"Sir, it's a world of hackers, so there's your answer."

"We may need to shut the entire thing down," one of the agents thinks aloud.

"That might not be advisable, sir."

"Why not?" the director asks.

"We have a few theories as to what could happen."

"Such as?"

"Trigger a forced reboot of the Grid and the Net, damage the Data Stream."

"How could that happen?"

"It's automatic, sir. If integrity dips below a certain level, if the power is drained to a certain level, any number of Grid protocols will trigger."

"Those protocols are for a catastrophic event during the time of war. Has a forced reboot ever happened?"

The men look at each other for a moment, thinking.

"We've had simulations, but never an actual event."

"Then shut down this Babylon now."

"Sir, we can't do that."

"What? Why?"

"Babylon is a world on the Net. It exists everywhere and nowhere. That's what we're telling you, sir. To shut down Babylon means shutting down the nation's Grid, the Net. It's illegal to do so, per the Rule of Law, Supreme Senate, and executive edict. Not even the President of the United States can order it. The power and the Net must always be on."

Babylon, the Net
Time: Unclear

"I can't take it anymore," Malaria's holo-identity freezes in place. "I have to unplug." The plague cloud that he had transformed into begins to coalesce back into a human form.

"You can't do it," Tapeworm pleads.

"I can't do it. Forty-five hours. I need to sleep. I know what happens. You sleep-wake. You have hallucinations. You lose the ability to know what's real and what's a dream. Your damn brain could shut down and force your body into a coma."

"Take more drugs," Surge's voice says. "That's what they are probably doing."

"No. I can't risk it. I have two important jobs coming up. I'm unplugging. The Jew-Christians beat me." His holo-identity vanishes.

"I'm never leaving," Surge says. "Never!"

Tapeworm stands on the top of a skyscraper, looking for them. The entire city is burning with a black sky firing lightning bolts at the ground. Rivers of lava are flowing through the streets and the sky is also filled with giant mosquitoes courtesy of Malaria, but they are disappearing now that he has unplugged.

"Tapeworm," a voice says.

He spins around and a miniature version of Zen stands behind him.

"If you give me the data I need, we'll spare you."

"Spare me." He laughs. "What does that mean? We control the Babylon mains."

"But we control the Grid."

"That's a lie."

"Ghost in the machine," a voice says.

Tapeworm's legs begin to melt into the ground. "Stop! How are you doing that?" His arms melt away and his entire body is dissolving.

"Just give me the data and I'll stop them. Goli and NIS are savages, you know. They know what your true fear is."

"I have no fears."

"Tapeworm, there is no human without a true fear. Most have many. Help me save you."

"I have no fears at all. I am the greatest tek-hunter ever. There is no one I can't find and no one I can't eventually capture or destroy. I have the stats to prove it."

"I need to download all government black ops files on code name Red Hat Man. We have them already, but we think your bosses are trying to be clever by storing the data in files we've already hacked, thinking we would have crossed them off our list."

"I'm a tek-hunter, not a hacker, unless the hack is to hunt." Half of Tapeworm's body has dissolved. "How are you doing this? If I can't figure it out, I'll just reset Babylon—again and again. You'll never be able to do this trick again and I'll figure out how you're doing it too."

"I'm sorry."

"Sorry?"

"We have the data already."

"What?"

"It was just meant to distract you. It's done."

"What?"

Outlands, State of Puerto Rico
5:12 p.m., 19 October 2096

An obese man sitting sandwiched in a pod-chair rips his VR helmet from his face, yanking the ocular connectors off too.

"Owww!" he yells. He looks around his studio dwelling, squinting and disorientated. The apartment is filled with garbage everywhere. "No!" He strains to grab his VR helmet. "I got to get back in. Computer, reconnect! Reconnect!"

"Access denied." The voice comes from the apartment's ceiling speakers.

"Reconnect!"

"Access denied."

"No!" The man's eyes become teary and he starts to panic, looking all around. "Where is it? Where is it?!" He begins to pry himself out of the pod-chair.

"You're Tapeworm."

The man looks up in shock. Every monitor in the apartment has a different face looking back at him.

"You're the great Tapeworm? The great tek-assassin. You're disgusting looking," one of the kids say.

"No! Computer disconnect all vid-feeds!"

"Access denied."

"No!" The man tries to shield his face with his hands. "Don't look at me!"

The faces on the vid-screens start to laugh.

"You need to eat some tapeworms, you fat pig. To eat all that blubber you're carrying."

"Don't look at me!" he pulls his dirty top over his head.

"I always thought you were some skinny kid tekkie or a hot babe. But look at you."

"Don't trust the feed, man. Until you meet 'em, you could be talking to Pellet's momma."

The teks start to laugh again.

"No, your momma."

"Tapeworm is so ugly that you couldn't pay the ugliest sex worker who'll work for free to get with him."

They all laugh again.

He manages to get out of his pod-chair. "Don't look at me!" He sloshes through the garbage of the apartment, and he throws the front door open.

"Tapeworm is a hoarder pig, too."

"I'm so disappointed right now. It's like the original Darth Vader taking off his head mask and seeing the face of Pellet's momma."

"No, it's like seeing the real Tapeworm crying like an asexual, saying 'don't look at me!'"

Tapeworm runs out of the apartment, almost tripping. The teks can't stop laughing and making fun of him

Moments later, they hear a loud crash outside from the street.

"What was that noise? Was that a crash?"

Wildlands, Alaska
5:13 p.m., 19 October 2096

An eyeball is watching him—a tiny domestic drone from the other side of a side window.

A boy of no more than a hundred pounds is sitting in a pod-chair with all kinds of wires attached to the top of his VR helmet. He taps his helmet, with its brain-reading tek now disconnecting, and he picks it off his head.

"Tapeworm, you fool!" he says to himself. "That was their play all along. Auto-set Babylon."

He leaps out of his pod-chair

"Which means I gotta get out of here."

The door of his loft apartment crashes open. Surge dashes to a table with an assortment of guns. He's grabbed and forcibly thrown across the room and smashes into the wall. He slowly sits up trembling, tears streaming from his eyes.

"Nice to meet you, Surge the Purge. I'm Goli, the tek-lord," the giant says. "Reality hurts, doesn't it?" He grabs the boy again, swings him back, and then body slams him to the floor. "You got friends of mine jailed and tortured by the government. I'm going to stomp your ribs in and then I'm going to ask you a series of questions…once."

Another man appears behind him—NIS, smiling. "The list of top tek-lords in the world is getting smaller." His glasses sparkle with electric charges. "Surge, have you ever been electrocuted before. I have quite a long list of requests from my colleagues." A blue electric charge flies from his glasses and shocks the boy. "That's for the Christians." Another shock. "That's for the Jews." Another shock. "That's for the Catholics." Another shock. "That's for the Mormons." The boy tries to scramble away across the floor, but is shocked again with larger charges.

"Please! I will tell you anything you want. Let me live! Please!"

Goli grabs him by the waist of his pants. "NIS is so nice. This is how I talk to people I hate. He flings him across the room. Surge smashes into data towers, breaking them to pieces, and the power cuts off in a quarter of the room.

"Let me live! Please!" Surge pleads, his body convulsing from shock and his mouth bleeding.

Ad-Hoc Situation Room, Non-Public Off-Site Offices, Washington, DC
7:02 p.m., 19 October 2096

The director has his entire Homeland Cyber-Division leadership assembled.

"Aren't these VR worlds just sex? How can sex addicts cripple the nation's Grid?" the director asks.

"Yes, sir. Sex, drugs, but also criminal activities and Anarchist terrorist plotting. But there is also a significant population who just 'live' there."

"Live?" the director asks.

"Holo-communities of their choosing. In the past, the future, Mars, other planets."

"How many people are connected now?"

"About two hundred and fifty million, sir."

The director looks at him with astonishment, almost not knowing what to say. "A third of America's population is in there now? That can't be accurate."

"Not everyone is fully plugged in or fully engaged. They could be running it on a console or device in the background while they're doing something else."

"Why can't we cut the connection? I don't accept what I was told earlier."

"Think of it as hundreds of millions of individuals each signing on from hundreds of millions of different points, sir. The only way to sever the link is to shut off the entire nation Grid, which is impossible to do."

"How are they using this much power? It's a VR world. How could sex shows, playing vid-games, and running around in simulated holo-communities be using that much power?"

"Interface, sir. The VR doesn't use much at all, but people interfacing with their devices and systems do. Their holo-identities could be connected to all their vid and data lines so they can still make and receive calls and texts. They might interface with their house so it can make their food and feed them while they're in, they could be in while they're driving…"

"Okay, I understand. I need solutions people. The power drain must be stopped—now. I'm new so a promotion goes to the first person who gives me that solution."

The staffers look at each other.

"Sir, I'm sorry, but there's no other way to solve it."

"I'm supposed to tell the president, Congress, Homeland, and the Supreme Senate that the only solution to this cyber threat is to literally send the United States of America into darkness?"

"It wouldn't be a long period of time, sir."

"That's what you want me to tell them."

"Yes. It's either that or the power consumption will grow and the Grid's fail-safes will do it anyway."

He pounds the desk. "There has to be another way! Is this the best we can do?"

"Sir, we could send out teams to each of the Grid hubs and manually disconnect them, then re-connect them."

"Won't that shut the entire thing down too?"

"No, sir, it would be a managed and regional shutdown, not total. I believe every disconnected hub would simply reinitialize. While it did that, we'd have the A.I. go in, re-create and re-establish new firewalls instantaneously. Firewalls they won't have bypass or back-door codes for."

"It won't work," another deputy says.

The director ignores him and looks at the other deputy again. "How sure are you that this will work?"

"It's never been done before, but I am ninety percent sure it will work."

"Do it then."

Midwest Deserts, Oklahoma
8:41 p.m., 19 October 2096

The shadow-jet slows to a near stop fifteen feet in the air and a squad of black-clad men jump from the side cargo door. The jet is long gone when the men's feet touch the desert ground and their base-jump parachutes retract back into their backpacks. One of them kneels and types on his wrist console and a section of the open desert begins to descend.

8:45 p.m.

Ten of the men stand, pointing their tek-rifles out, in a circle. Three other men are at the console tower typing in commands to the moving keyboard on a dark screen.

"I'm in," one of the black-clad teks says to his other squad members.

Another touches his ear-set. "We're in…yes…we'll do the hard reset now." He nods to the tek.

The tek hits a button on the side of the machine.

There is an explosion.

Power in the nearest tek-cities shut down. People in the streets are panicking, but then the power returns.

**Ad-Hoc Situation Room, Non-Public Off-Site Offices, Washington, DC
12:02 a.m., 20 October 2096**

The director reviews the files on his tablet. "What happened?"

"Homeland confirmed it. Our bounty hunters were after two of the top ten cyber-terrorists on the Most Wanted Registry."

"What happened?"

"We don't know. They tracked them into Babylon…or they came across them in Babylon, we're not clear yet. There was a confrontation and then this incident happened—"

"I still don't understand how a VR world on the Net can threaten the nation's Grid when we control the Net and the Grid. Where are they? Have we really lost all three? Three of our best cyber-terrorist trackers?"

"One is confirmed dead. We're investigating if he accidentally walked into traffic or committed suicide or was possibly chased by other unknown assailants."

"Walked into traffic? You can't walk into oncoming traffic. The vehicles would stop automatically. Suicide. The other two?"

"They've disappeared."

"That's it?"

"We have every resource looking for them. If there is any kind of interaction with the system—death, arrest, accident—we'll know. Their true bios went into the system and we're notified of any flags. We never knew their real identities by design. He could have been pushed into traffic, sir."

"He killed himself. We have no leads whatsoever on the other two?"

"They must have been captured or they're hiding off-Grid."

"These were our best hunters?"

"The best, sir. Our own tek-lords, to use common speak."

"Does this cripple the cyber-terrorist bounty hunter program?"

"No, but…it means we'll probably never catch the uber-hackers or top tek-lords out there for the foreseeable future. Until we recruit others, and the good ones will take longer to catch."

"I just start the job and this is what I'm handed. I don't even get my honeymoon period."

"There's another matter. But we can discuss later."

"Discuss what later?"

"I'll bring it to you if we have more."

"You might as well give me all the bad news all together. I wouldn't be surprised if I get sacked over all this. There always has to be a fall guy for something like this."

"I hope that doesn't happen, sir. This wasn't your fault. We should put the blame with Homeland. It was their op. It actually wasn't anyone's fault."

"We don't want to tell them that. They like to think there is nothing that they can't control. When will the report be on my desk?"

"The field investigations are in process. We can have it to you in forty-eight hours. But if you want to know what really happened, it will take longer."

"I want to know what happened. Do both. The first report for the bosses. The real one for me. Assuming I keep the job."

"Yes, sir."

The Ant-Hill, Unknown Location, America
8:30 p.m., 19 October 2096

Moses, Sek, Niccolo, Mr. Blond, and a very pregnant Shoshana wait. The elevator opens and Goli, NIS, and Zen exit. Goli glances at his wife, Shoshana—she used to be completely bald before marriage, but now the "warrior" leader of the Jew's elite security force, the Wolf-Pack, keeps her hair very short. A large Star of David dangles from her necklace, dressed in black fatigues and combat boots, and "14051948" tattooed on her left forearm—the date the state of Jewish Israel was formed. With the Fall of Jewish Israel, the Solidarity tattoo became a common practice among many younger Jews, signifying a kind of blood oath that Jewish Israel would be rebuilt again by any means necessary. He gives a slight smile as he returns his attention back to the others.

Goli puts the data stick in Moses' hand.

Homeland Cyber-Threat & Terrorism Situation Room,
Washington, DC
9:02 a.m., 20 October 2096

The director leans forward in his chair and listens to the briefing of no less than the Senior Presidential Advisor—the man who first greeted him when he arrived in the District. Their deputies are also present, sitting quietly behind him. Normally it would be them briefing him, but everything about this Babylon incident is unusual.

"They were attacked in this Babylon VR world and attacked in the real world too," the Advisor continues.

"Has this ever happened in the history of the Cyber-Terrorist Division?" the director asks. "That operatives were compromised so completely. How were they found? I was told that we couldn't even locate them if we wanted to."

"We don't know how they were found. And we don't where the remaining two are. They were truly our best hunters, but they will be replaced."

"I've been given explicit instructions by the president and Homeland to locate and arrest every illegal hacker, tek-lord, cyber-pirate, cyber-terrorist there is. My job just got ten times harder. The ones they were after were Jew-Christians, correct?"

"Yes, that's what we've been able to determine."

"Are our problems still Jew-Christians?" the director asks.

"Jew-Christians? You're behind the times. No. They left the tek-cities two decades ago or more. They so rarely show up on the reports anymore that it's like they don't exist. No, our number one problem domestically is the Anarchists. The Jew-Christians are far away in the Trog-land territories and are as quiet as mice."

"Mice aren't quiet. What are they doing out there? I don't believe that they are just living."

"To date, we have no reports to the contrary."

"What was this Babylon incident about then? Was it really a random chance encounter? We also have an entire tactical squad in the hospital and I don't believe the explosion was some accident with the Grid station."

"Regardless, the team was not killed and the explosion accomplished the same objective—allowed us to begin the Grid reset," another man says.

"Where does that leave us then?" the director asks.

"That the new Babylon will be operational by the end of the week."

The director shakes his head. "How can a stupid VR world be so important? Every news feed is saturated with reports on it. You'd think the planet was about to be hit by a moon-sized asteroid with the panic among the public."

"There has been a dramatic spike in suicides," one of the deputies says.

The director shakes his head again. "I had the Surgeon General march into my new office at 6 a.m. today yelling at me that the restoration of this VR world was a matter of national security."

"It would have been operational within a day," the advisor continues, "but Homeland is making sure that this incident can never be repeated. No one will be able to alter the reality of the Babylon environment like they did here. They'll never be able to take over the programming commands for the entire VR world. Other VR worlds will be following our same protocols."

The director leans back in his chair. "What else? Why are you here, really?"

"We may have a problem."

"What problem?"

"We do agree with you. There is a high probability that this whole 'battle' in Babylon was a ruse."

"To do what?"

The advisor looks at one of his deputies, who stands. "They may have changed something."

"Changed something?" the director asks.

"Changed something in the Data Stream."

"We don't know what they changed," the Advisor says, "but we believe that it happened."

"But we avoided any real damage or compromise to critical systems?"

"Yes."

"Was there damage or compromise to auxiliary systems?"

"No."

"Then what do you base your suspicions on?"

"It happened before."

"What? The Net has been hacked before? When?"

"At least once before. Maybe one other time."

"When was the last time?"

"Twenty years ago."

"What happened then?"

"It was the day after Kansas Event."

The director is quiet for a moment.

"I'm sorry. I know you lost family there."

"What do you think they did? These Jew-Christians."

"They changed something."

"What? How do you know?"

"We don't know. It's a complicated process of monitoring data volumes, etcetera. Something is different…we think."

"You think? What?"

"There's literally no way to know," the advisor's deputy answers. "With trillions, quadrillions, quintillions of data flowing through the Net, there is no way to know, and we will never know. We only monitor the Grid, but that is only four percent of the total DataStream."

"What could they have done? And to go through all this."

"It would have taken years to set up for," the advisor says.

"Absolutely mind-boggling all the steps they would have had to go through, much of it seemingly impossible."

"The first time you said it happened was after—"

"The Kansas Event."

"Coincidence?"

"We don't think so."

"Then you believe it was the Jew-Christians. Not some foreign power?"

"The Anarchists don't have the tek-skills and don't have the patience for such a long play. Foreign powers? Maybe, but they'd have other things on their mind than altering the general Net."

"Why would the Jew-Christians hack the Net and make changes then? They hate everything about the Grid and tek society."

The advisor shrugs his shoulders. "We don't know."

"Do you suspect something dangerous?"

"Maybe. But let's say they changed a history file. The Allies lost WW II and Nazi Germany won. Clearly that's too well-known, but let's say that. It would affect the culture and ripple out from there. And we would never know the truth because we weren't there and…no one keeps ancient analog files or physical paper files or physical books anymore."

"Except Jew-Christians." The director thinks for a moment. "So the belief is that they changed something that could change our very culture?"

"Our future," the advisor says.

One of the deputies adds, "Sirs, we reviewed every possible Net file we could think of, but we found nothing. It's not historical, political, or religious. We simply don't know. We looked at all the obvious things such as the president's biographical data, etcetera— even though it's accessible, it's protected. We have firewalls on all core files. Then we checked all elected officials, past and present, their staff, world leaders, corporations, NGOs, organizations, every possible thing we could think of, but sirs, that's just it. We looked at everything *we* could think of, not what they'd think of. Our minds don't work like theirs. We could look for a million years and never figure out the data they targeted, and again, if they successfully changed it, we'd never know."

"And you can't back up the Net's Data Stream," another deputy says. "The sum total of all the data flowing back and forth through the Net—text, vids, audio, code. That would be a data bank the size of the planet."

"The Net is an ocean and you can't bottle the ocean."

"Exactly."

"So we'll never know what they did."

The advisor corrects him. "We *will* know, but unfortunately we'll never know that we know. It's like those time travel movies about changing something in time and it changes reality. When that reality is changed, you will never know there was another reality that existed before the change."

"Talk about a conspiracy," the director says, shaking his head.

The Finger of God

The White House
9:26 a.m., 23 October 2096

"Chess Master is moving," the Secret Service agent says into his ear-set, standing at his hallway post.

Four-term President T. Wilson appears, followed by two agents to his office. His re-election to a fifth term next month is a certainty, surpassing the record of Franklin Delano Roosevelt set 151 years ago.

Zhongnanhai Presidential Palace, Beijing, China
9:45 a.m., 23 October 2096

President Ri Wen, the premier of China and the leader of the Chinese-Indian Alliance (CHIN). It was the previous reign of his father which created the union with India to form the Alliance and ushered in the decline of the Russian Bloc, and the cessation of Caliphate incursions into CHIN territories.

The president walks to the comm-room followed by an entourage of staffers, aides, and military leaders.

Murabba Presidential Palace, Riyadh, Saudi Arabia
9:55 a.m., 23 October 2096

The Emperor Al-Siddiq rules the Supreme Islamic Caliphate and during his reign expanded their Islamic territorial conquests with the Fall of Jewish Israel and into Africa—though the African Collective stopped their expansion in the Islamic-Christian War. He also issued the order for the total destruction of Palestine Israel—the main Muslim antagonists within the Islamic empire. His late father led the Fall of Western Europe—twenty countries seized by the new Caliphate decades ago with millions of people fleeing, those fortunate enough to escape.

The Emperor walks to his Supreme offices, followed by an entourage of sheiks.

Oval Office, The White House
10:00 a.m., 23 October 2096

President T. Wilson greets each of his fellow heads of state, two vid-screens attached to the Oval Office walls with faces staring back at him—Ri-Wen on the left and the Emperor on the other screen.

"Thank you, gentlemen, for attending. I must confess that I got the idea for our own little summit from the late President Krutikov. Where he failed, I want us to continue forward for our mutual benefit. No one, even in my own administration, knows of my plan, and you, gentlemen, will be the first to hear the name of the program. I wish for this to be a joint global initiative—the Sphere Program. It will allow us to solve multiple problems that each of our empires face. Catapult our nations and our people into the future. This goes far beyond the urban retrofitting of our tek-cities. Consider this: macro-adaptable, generational architecture.

The smart-cities we build today, we build for the next fifty years and the next five hundred years. America is also not the only nation with an Anarchist and Separatist problem. The ability to protect our people from terrorism in any form, natural disasters—earthquakes, flood, hurricanes, natural pandemics, global atmospheric change, and global continental shift. The ability to manage our people in our cities—population control and growing energy needs. The ability to deal with those populations outside our tek-cities—all of them.

"And then there is the insatiable energy needs of our populations. My people are telling me the same thing yours are—at some point the demands of infrastructure will so far outstrip our ability to meet that even with our energy resources that we risk an energy crash and our Grids shut down. Cities cannot be run by people anymore. But Sphere can. If we can work out the details, specific to our own regions, then we can roll Sphere out globally as a unified coalition."

"Would America take credit for this initiative?" President Wen asks.

"The world's three superpowers would," Wilson answers.

"Why would you do this?" the Emperor asks.

"You know why. We all know the answer. We all face the same problems. One of our regions destabilizes, it will destabilize the other two. We all know what I mean. In fact, the three of us are probably the only three people on the planet who do."

"I'm intrigued by the notion that you have added population management to the initiative," Wen says.

"America has a half-trillion people," Wilson says. "That's not counting the people outside the tek-cities. Population management must be part of it."

The Emperor says, "My people do not have the trust in

machines that you do, but I am also intrigued. Why do you feel this has to be a joint effort among us?"

"We're already working together jointly on the Earth Asteroid Defense programs. We were looking at expanding that cooperation at Krutikov's Summit. We even secretly worked together on our combined problem with the Internationalists. The Sphere Program makes sense, but it can only work if we all do it jointly. Doing so separately would be too threatening to the other two."

3:45 p.m.

President T. Wilson sits with his back to the bay window at his Executive desk, satisfied with the day. Five aides, male and female, sit on the adjacent chairs to form an upside-down "U" formation.

"What are sources saying?" Wilson asks one of his aides.

"The Sphere Program is well-received, though they're trying to figure out if you have some private agenda to make them look foolish or if you're trying to take something from them."

Wilson smiles a bit. "That's expected. I want both teams on the first flight to Beijing and Riyadh tomorrow. Work with their people on all the details."

"Is there a time deadline, sir?"

"Say next spring or summer of next year, but tell them that I would like to inform my media sometime during my first one hundred days of my fifth term."

"You did it, sir." The aide grins. "Two weeks away and you'll officially surpass FDR as the longest-serving president. Well-deserved, sir."

"Thank you, but first, let the people get their chance to vote next month."

"Of course, sir."

"Get the teams moving."

"Yes, sir."

The aide stands and exits the office. Wilson turns to senior advisors seated.

"Thoughts?" Wilson asks.

"Do we really want to get in bed with these two, sir? They're going to try to steal all our tek. Especially the CHINs."

Wilson smiles. "We're only using the tek they've already stolen."

"You asked me for an updated report on the Trog-land territories, and you're right, of course. Our intel is positive more attacks are planned."

"More attacks are always planned and always coming."

"I miss the days of the Jew-Christians, sir."

"This is the Jew-Christians. I'm positive this is all being orchestrated by them."

"We have no proof of that, sir."

"I don't need proof to know what I know. Remember, I wrote the original threat memo on the subject before I was even Director of Homeland. What we have is a whole soup of sedition outside our tek-cities, religious and atheistic both. I never said our only threat was the Jew-Christians and Muslims. I was playing long-tail chess. Destroy the threat in the far future, then move to the near future and then end with the current. My strategy worked. The Jew-Christians are gone from the cities, the Muslims are gone— except for Michigan, the Anarchists are gone, all outside our cities. Purity.

"I have no doubt the Jew-Christians have been stirring up the Anarchists against us. Though the Anarchists were the way they are long before the two came into contact with each other. But we still have informants embedded."

"I do like the Sphere Program, sir. Leave them all out there, and as we continue with Sphere, keep monitoring, and watch their populations shrink. Cut off their access to the tek-cities."

"Or they leave. The Star Trek religionists went to Canada, Jedis are confined to Northern California, Vampires migrated to Europa, and all the others went to India or somewhere else off the continent."

"What about Michigan? The Caliphate spy-state in our own country."

"We'll never have to worry. If there ever is a war, they would receive the first strike. That's sufficient incentive for them to behave themselves."

"But we'll have to pull out all our infiltration teams."

Wilson gives him a look. "Why?"

"There would be no way to get the data back to us."

There is a muffled knock at the door and the president's secretary appears. "Sir," he says.

"Yes."

"You have a phone call, sir. It's President Wen."

Wilson says to the aide, "Leave them there. We'll figure out ways for them to get the intel to us." He rises from his seat, walks to his Executive desk, and pushes a button on a red dome device.

"President Wen, long time, no talk. How may I be of assistance?"

There is a long pause on the line. "Hello, Chess Master."

Everyone notices the expression on the president's face change to hate. He signals to his staff to get the Secret Service. Everyone freezes as they listen to the unknown voice—unknown to all, except the president.

"No words of welcome for your ol' friend? If I told them that Mr. Fournier Gangrene wishes to speak with the Chess Master, I don't think they would have accommodated us."

Secret Service burst into the Oval Office. The lead agent shakes his head.

They can hear a breath before the voice comes through the speaker phone.

"We had this conversation before, didn't we? Back in May '76. Funny. That's twenty years ago. After the Event. I told you then to leave us alone. Now I find out that you are at it again. You found the Red Hat Man and killed him. We found the man who killed the Red Hat Man and killed him. You'll find him soon enough. So you wish to play with us again."

The three Secret Service agents are standing next to the president.

"The Finger of God always trumps the Hand of the Five Cities," the voice continues. "Do you know how we always find out? How we know what you're doing? You think it's because we have clever tek-lords or spies buried deep within your administration. No, Galerius. It's you. You're our spy. We have tek that's calibrated to your brain waves alone. That's what the Red Hat Man did. Once you step outside, we can download data, memories even, straight from your brain. You're looking for spies when all along we've been literally reading your mind. The historical Galerius died a horrific death and so will you. Because our machine can also reverse the waves to erase your entire mind and trigger necrosis in every cell in your body. Build your Sphere Program, Galerius. Build it as fast as you can."

The line disconnects.

Everyone stares at each other dumbfounded.

"Sir, did that terrorist really call you before?" a Secret Service agent asks.

"We couldn't trace the call, sir," another agent says.

"Mr. President, I swear it was Beijing. All the codes were genuine." The presidential secretary's face is pale with worry.

"It obviously wasn't Beijing, which means they have our comm codes," the lead agent says.

"Who's Galerius, Mr. President?" another agent asks.

"I am!" Wilson shouts. "Why can't we trace that call? This is the White House of the United States of America. Trace that call!"

The Ant-Hill, Unknown Location, America
3:50 p.m., 23 October 2096

Moses' eyes open.

M watches her husband as he unplugs from his VR pod and stands from the chair. They are the only two in the small, private comm room; the walls and ceilings are in constant holographic flux.

"Why did you do that?" she asks. "The man will spend every waking moment trying to find our brain-reading machine in the District that doesn't exist."

"He doesn't know that."

"We all miss Elder Mother Esther. We'll continue missing your mother, every bit as much as your father, Atticus. But I have to ask, because you're not just my husband, you're a Founder, a leader in our Order. Both of us are. Are your decisions sound?"

"If you're asking if they're free of emotion, the obvious answer is no. I get enraged at the murder of my parents as I do every October and May, as I will every year 'til I die. If you're asking if the decisions are sound, then the answer is yes. The safety of the Protestant Order and the entire Continuum is always foremost in my mind in everything I do. But I know my 'ol' friend' better than any profiler we have. He'll do a lot more than just rip the District apart to see if there was any truth to my lies. It is just the beginning until we get approval."

"Then I have good news." She smiles at him. "Retaliation has been approved by the Continuum."

Moses raises his arms up in the air. "And the angels looked up in jubilation and cried out in unison, Amen."

The Rise of Brazil Khan

The Palácio do Planalto, Brasília, Brazil
11:12 a.m., 24 October 2096

A young female receptionist stands nervously in the waiting room, constantly glancing at the closed door. Sister Serena admires the artwork on the walls, taking them all in with her one good eye, the other behind her black eye patch. She is dressed casually—no habit or any other nun attire.

The door opens and Mr. Khan enters with two guards. He gestures with his head at the receptionist, who walks past them out the door.

"Is it Sister Serena or are you using your terrorist name, Sister Cyclops?" he asks.

Serena doesn't turn around to acknowledge them, but keeps her gaze locked on one particular painting—a celebrating crowd at Brazil's giant Jesus statue monument (Christ the Redeemer) in Rio de Janeiro.

"I'm surprised you haven't burned this one," she says to him. "But I'm sure you'll get around to it. In fact, I'm surprised your country hasn't blown the statue up like Muslims do, but I'm sure you'll get around to that too. To answer your question, do you believe in the enslavement of women and men for the use and pleasure of degenerates, Mr. Khan?"

"That is an offensive thing to ask. I am staunchly anti-slavery. My own mother was an escaped slave—forced into prostitution—and my own biological father is an open question, as they say. But you know that already."

Sister Serena turns to face him. "As you haven't forgotten your heritage, the answer to your own question is already answered."

"I never did think I would see you again, Sister Serena. You are either bold, or foolish, to walk into the Presidential Palace alone. You church people are so clever with your plots. You've caused quite an embarrassment for our president. Fortunately for you he is not here, but that is why you're so being so bold. What do I owe this visit to? And is it too part of some larger church plot?"

"You can send your bodyguards away. If I wanted to kill you, they sure as hell wouldn't be able to stop me."

The security men are visibly angered by the insult, but Khan dismisses them. The two men walk out the door, glaring at her, closing it behind them. He turns and Sister Serena is already sitting in a corner chair.

"Please sit, Mr. Khan."

Khan approaches cautiously and sits in the adjacent chair, a small table between them. She places a small disk on the table. The device nullifies their conversation to anyone or anything outside its immediate range.

"Privacy devices don't work here. Our listening devices are too good."

"It's not a privacy device."

Khan looks at the device again.

"Do you know about the Sphere Program?"

Khan leans back. "Is that why you're here? To try to stir some dissension between Brazil and the superpowers? It will not work. Brazil does not want to be a part of any coalition of Chinese, Muslim, and American dogs."

"Do you know what Sphere really is?"

"What is it you're trying to do? You're an anti-slaver terrorist. Why are you trying to be some kind of geo-political agent provocateur? You are much better at killing criminals and comforting prostitutes than trying to play high-stakes statecraft. You should stick to your strengths."

"It's the first step."

"I will not play your game."

"Are you involved?"

His eyes narrow. "Involved in what?"

"With the impostor in your Presidential Palace."

"I have no idea what you mean or what game you're playing."

"That's what happened in Russia. They wanted to do it to Krutikov."

"Do what?"

She stands from her chair. "I'm here because you're the only one inside the government who is not part of the inner circle. Being born of a prostitute has limited your political potential."

"I am immune to such insults."

"Take your most loyal men to the Presidential Palace, bring a doctor, geneticist, and blood specialist with you, and arrest him. You will have to kill some of his guards, but that can't be helped. Do a full bio-scan and biopsy of the 'Turtle' and see for yourself. But be prepared for the shock. It's no longer science fiction."

Khan laughs. "I don't believe anything you're saying. Why are you telling me this?"

"You're my enemy. They're my enemy. I want to see my enemies kill each other. Both of you can't survive. Only one. Let's see if you're as good as you think you are. Let's see if you're ready to be a superpower too. Or if you wish to remain a pathetic, anti-religious communications deputy to die in obscurity as other empires use your nation as the pawn in their own global game."

"And what will you do while this all happens?"

"Mr. Khan, we will not be watching the battle. We find you as uninteresting as a speck of dust floating through the air. You said so yourself—we're church people, so our interests are faith and family. You are neither. We tell you because the chaos will be a benefit to us and a cover to us as we rectify the same problem in Mexico. However, do stay away from us. Leave us alone and you will never see or hear from us again. The Slave Wars are over. Good luck, Mr. Khan. And don't pretend you and your people don't suspect it already or haven't suspected it for years. I've just given you the confirmation."

Serena rises from the chair and walks to the Christ the Redeemer painting on the wall. "Can I have this picture? I know you're going to burn it or something. I know just the place in my church for it. I have quite a collection of paintings of religious monuments and churches from all over the Spanish Americas."

"Take it."

"Thank you, Mr. Khan."

She removes the painting from the wall and starts towards the door. It opens and the two bodyguards re-enter the room and hold the door open.

"Bye, Mr. Khan."

She leaves with the big painting.

Khan stands from his seat and looks at the disk she left on the table.

"She left it behind," one of the guards says.

"Pick it up," he directs.

The guards look at one another and one slowly picks up the disk. He considers the weight in his hand, shakes it a bit, and then pulls it closer to his face.

"How did she get this device inside the building?" Khan asks.

"It's not made of anything dangerous," the guard answers and slides it open. Inside is a circular pouch with something written on it.

"What does it say?"

The guard looks up at him surprised.

"'Original genetic material of Joaquim Jimenas.' That's the president. What does this mean, Mr. Khan? Original genetic material?"

Khan grabs it from the guard's hand.

Oval Office, The White House
6:01 p.m., 23 October 2096

The Homeland assistant deputy director stands in front of the seated president at his desk. The room is filled with other agents, staffers, and advisors.

"We did find our agent dead, but it was ruled as an accident."

"How?" the president asks.

"He fell down a flight of stairs. Broke his neck. But it was in a public place."

"What do you want done, sir?"

The president folds his arms. "I want every deep-background agent working on this. Have them identify all the terrorists' leadership. No." He looks away. "We're not going to play into their panic. Monitor and we'll move the Sphere Program forward, ahead of schedule."

"Yes, sir."

"Make it impossible for those not in the tek-cities to move in and out of the tek-cities."

"Outlands too?"

"Use our eminent domain statutes and start—quietly, complete media black-out—acquiring all of their territory. There will be no Outlands—just the outer perimeter areas of the cities."

"They'll have their lawyers on us," an advisor speaks up.

"The beauty of being the president is that we can nullify their lawsuits—national security. They don't like it, then they can go live with the Anarchists in the wastelands."

"We should also consider having Jew-Christian experts on staff, sir," another aide says.

"We did that before," another says. "Those JCs, Rabbi Susan and Bishop Joe. A total disaster. We moved three steps forward and ten steps back."

The president ignores them. "I'm the expert on religious people in this administration. These terrorists will not direct this administration's actions, but it will suffer from them. I want the Homeland Director and Joint Chiefs assembled."

Department of Homeland Defense and Intelligence Agency Security Dispatch / 25 October 2096

Notify POTUS that the Minister of Communications, Vinicius Khan, has seized control of the Brazilian government in a coup. The Brazilian president and all the federal cabinet are all unaccounted for and assumed in custody.

The Kremlin, Moscow, Russia
9:16 p.m., 25 October 2096

The KGB head, Zukov, waits with his four aides in the room. They sit around a simple table in a dimly-lit room. The dark-haired men are all dressed in dark uniforms, but Zukov is older and visibly more threatening, like some kind of crime boss.

"What do you think of my recommendation?" the aide asks.

"This Sphere Program of the Americans is our only focus now," Zukov answers.

"We must find a way to get into their program, use the Brazilian situation to our advantage."

"And what do you suggest we do? Barricade people in the cities? Kill anyone who sets up some community, small or large, outside the cities? This is a large planet and cities take up only a tiny fraction of it, no matter how large we make our skyscrapers or how massive our cities grow. There will always be people outside of the cities. We monitor and take action when we need to and that's it."

"And is the president simply going to ignore the Americans' program?" another man asks.

"Whether he does or doesn't, there will be some program. We need some version of the Sphere Program not against the people, but against the Americans, Chinese, and Muslims—that's who the president had to detonate a bomb against. They're the ones trying to invade our nation and kill and enslave our people. What a bunch of religionists in Europa do means nothing. We can quash them whenever we want."

"Zukov, be careful," an aide warns. "It is official Presidential policy—"

"Not all religionists are the same," Zukov says. "They are not our threat. Not anymore. We purged them from the government. It's finished. This is a real threat."

"These religions in Russia are a threat."

"They are Russian. They are Europan. Their loyalty is to the Russian Bloc."

"Just because we know good ones, doesn't mean anything."

"It means enough to me."

"But Zukov—" The man stops himself.

Zukov stares at him. "You weren't about to make the severe political mistake of mentioning my ex-wife?"

"No, sir. I would never do such a foolish thing."

"Good, I know you to be smarter than that. Besides, we can't watch everyone, but our machines can. We pick the threats we focus on. The religionists are not that threat, despite American and Chinese propaganda to the contrary. It's the superpowers—these super-thugs of the planet."

"We must do everything we can to elevate our own power to join them on the world stage, as it was in the past."

Zukov nods. "Exactly. That is what the president feels. That is what I feel. The Glory of Great Russia. When we were feared by our own people and everyone else."

"Zukov, why are we here waiting for the president?"

"Does it matter? He calls, we come. That's all there is to it."

The communication device on the table activates. Every man at the table has a look of fear.

"Zukov." The voice is low with a deep menacing bass.

"Yes, Mr. President."

"I need you to place a call."

The Palácio do Planalto, Brasília, Brazil
Noon, 26 October 2096

Brazil Khan enters his office—the Presidential office—and sits down in front of the desk phone. He pauses for a moment and then picks it up.

"President Khan here."

There is a long pause. "Congratulations, newly appointed President Khan. I like men who seize what they want—they are real men. I thought you were an effeminate academic that infests so many of the offices of heads of state. I see you can be ruthless…like a gangster should be. It's very difficult to impress a Russian gangster, but you have impressed me. To so completely seize power and execute all your opposition."

"You seem to know a lot about the internal workings of my country."

"Don't be naïve. Everyone does."

"What do I owe the pleasure of your call, President Igor?"

"What do you plan to do with your religious citizens?"

"Why? I thought you had called to talk about this Sphere Program. Why would you call me about them?"

"You are not to harm them. Exile them to a region of your country like we have done. Leave them alone and go about your business."

"Why would you take an interest in such a matter? It's beneath you."

"If you harm them, I will kill you."

Khan's expression changes to anger, but he says nothing. He listens, but, again, there is a long pause.

"I need them," Igor continues. "They must remain alive as the fail-safe for what I'm becoming. Separate them from your country, if you must, but leave them alone. Do I need to demonstrate my seriousness?"

"No, but I have every intention to marginalize them."

"I don't care about that. But you can't kill them. That means civil war. I can't take the chance that you'll kill them all. Neither of us can. They may even retaliate and kill you."

"I doubt that."

"Doubt whatever you want, but that's what will happen. Ignore them and I'll ignore you."

"Does that mean you'll ignore Brazilian forces within the Russian Bloc territory?"

"Don't be insulting. You set foot on my Russian continent and the people will kill you. Stay in your region and we'll stay in ours."

"Canada and America? Mexico, the Central Americas?"

"I care nothing about those places."

"Good, because Brazil will no longer be in the shadows, and, as of today, there will be four superpowers in this world, despite my nation's global enemies."

"I myself will continue to recede into the shadows. And President Khan?"

"Yes."

"There will be *five* superpowers in this world."

"I'm glad we could talk, President Igor."

"Yes, President Khan. Have a good day and a good life, since I don't expect us to ever converse again after I end this call."

Wolves of Exodus

**The Oval Office, The White House
11:01 a.m., 26 October 2096**

The Secret Service chief faces the president, who sits at his desk, staring out his bay windows.

"Access is like a fingerprint. Endless strings of changing algorithms," the chief says. "How did this designated terrorist get through to your Presidential secured line? Even if they did it before, twenty years ago, it is not the same as today. Every possible protocol is different, the tek is different, the security measures are different. Different meaning better. However, the breach was made and we're not able to trace the line.

"Sir, the only way the terrorist could have called in to your Presidential secure line, that we can speculate, is if they had a legitimate line and cloned it."

"What are you saying?" President T. Wilson asks.

"One of the superpowers gave it to them."

"Who? The CHINs? Caliphate?"

"We'll find out, sir."

The president swivels in his chair to look at him directly. "Seems logical. The only problem is that I don't believe for a second that either one of them would do that."

"Maybe someone within their administration."

"That I would believe. Or…once again they just cut through our impenetrable Net-security like they did twenty years ago."

"We'll follow every lead, sir, and find out which one."

The president swivels his chair around again to stare out the window. "You do that."

Trog-land, America
9:01 p.m., 25 October 2096

They said in the future, there would be no poverty, no homelessness, and no aimless masses. Everyone would live in shiny, silver cities and everyone would have purpose. The reality is a dark opposite outside the tek-metropolises.

Trog-land. The term originally described those territories outside the tek-cities where Luddites lived—those who were rebelling against mechanization in favor of a simpler, retro-life, but that was so many decades ago. The term now describes the vast stretches of untamed, outer wastelands; dangerous territories outside the tek-cities filled with Anarchists and all their sub-divisions—Nihilists, Hedonists, Space Cadets, Goths, drug Zombies, Nudists, and Space Cadets. Trogs—the people of Trog-land.

It is where no sane—or insane—tek-dweller would dare go with its rampant violence, murders, and rape gangs. In a nation where all drugs are legal and age-of-consent laws for sex had long been abolished, it was where those activities still illegal happened and were run. Trogs, namely Anarchists, had long surpassed Muslims as the chief culprits of domestic terrorism in America—though the government still painted all terrorism as religious-based.

It is also where the general public believes Jew-Christians live, but the government knows they live beyond Trog-land.

Hordes of Trogs surround the three-vehicle armored RV convoy with an assortment of attack vehicles—franken-cars, two-wheeled motor-bikes, three-wheelers, quads, attack Segways, and motorized rollerblades. The headlights of both the Trog hordes and the three trespassing vehicles illuminate the night sky.

Inside the lead RV, Stein and his fellow Exiles watch them through the tinted windows in fear. The Trogs are a sight to behold—most are half-naked, bodies pierced and tattooed everywhere, most wear inhaler mouth masks or nose tubes so their drug of choice can be continuously pumped into their bodies from backpacks or waist-belt distributors, lots of bald heads and spiky hair, lots of clawed gloves, lots of weapons. The RV slams to a stop—their path is completely blocked by Trog vehicles.

"We should never have done this!" one of the male Exiles yells. "What if they have laser weapons? Our shielding won't protect us."

"Give it time," Stein said.

"Time for what?" another asks.

"They wouldn't send us through Trog territory unprotected."

"Wouldn't they?" a female says. "It's payback. This is their way to kill us. Have these degenerates do it. Look at them. If they breach the vehicle, I'm committing suicide."

"Stop it. We're not being abandoned," Stein says.

Something hits the top of their RV and they all jump. Then another. They realize that the Trogs are throwing rocks at the vehicles.

"Oh God, I don't want to be here," another female Exile yells.

Stein looks around. "How many weapons do we have?"

"Weapons? There's hundreds of them out there. Oh no, what's this one doing?"

A Trog walks up to their RV and starts to urinate on it.

The voices of the other RV drivers come over the speakers. "We should run. We can't simply wait here to die!"

"This is what happens when you align with religious terrorists."

"Give it time," Stein yells. "They're coming."

Bright lights appear in the sky, blinding everyone, inside the RV and outside. The lights disappear. The Trogs stare up at the sky; the Exiles do the same from within their RVs.

The Trogs hear something approaching from the distance. As the sounds get louder, all of the headlights on every vehicle automatically get dimmer.

A grinning Anarchist yells, "They've remoted in. Change the frequency!"

The lights continue to dim, including those of the RVs.

"They're here," a Space Cadet says, pointing.

The figures come out of the night, all wearing black helmets and dressed in black. After a few moments, they see a faint glow from the center of their chests. As they near, symbols glow brighter on their leather uniforms—large crosses on each of them.

"Them," one of the Nihilists says.

Trogs scream and run at them to attack. One second. Bullets rip through every approaching Trog. Their bodies fall to the ground dead at the same time. Every other Trog stops and makes no movement.

The first one reaches them, covered from head to toe in helmet and uniform. "I'm Goth Lila of the Goth Christian Order. I thought we had a treaty." Her voice comes through the helmet's speaker.

"You're trespassing in our territory."

"They are with us and, therefore, under our protection. Do you intend to do something about it?"

"One day we'll come out to where you Jew-Christians live," another Trog says.

"And do what?"

"You killed our people. Go away," a Hedonist says. "I'm already bored."

"So am I," Goth Lila says. "Sound your retreat call."

"No," an Anarchist says.

"We both have the same enemy. But don't make us an enemy too. Sound your retreat call," she repeats.

"No," the Anarchist leader says.

The Anarchist next to him shoots the leader in the head. "We can't lose any more people. We need them to attack the city." He takes his laser wand from his belt and vigorously waves it around. "Move out!"

The Trog horde responds by breaking their circle formation around the RVs. The new Anarchist leader jumps back on his quad with four others and drives away. The entire horde heads back to their wasteland city leaving all the dead Trog bodies behind.

Goth Lila walks to the lead RV as her other people watch the hordes retreat. She knocks on the side door. It opens slowly and Stein peers out at her from inside.

"You will see a lighted vehicle. Follow it closely. When we near the compound our auto-drive will take over your controls."

"Okay," Stein says.

"We thought you were going to leave us out here to die," a woman behind him says.

"Should we have?" Goth Lila asks and then turns from them.

Stein closes and secures the door.

"This was a mistake," a man says. "We've put our fate in the hands of terrorists."

Stein yells, "Shut up, all of you! I have never met any of you before, but from the moment we've been together you've been complaining. I've never heard so much complaining. If you don't want to join Faith World, why are you here? I'm going to ask this once: Who wants to go back home?" He looks at all of them. "Can you hear me on the other RVs?" He waits for a response. "Well?"

"Yes," a voice from the second RV says.

"We hear you," the third RV says.

"I heard many of you refer to the Faithers as terrorists, which means you've completely drank the government propaganda. As a member of the courts for his entire life, let me tell you what the truth is and maybe you'll do me the mutual courtesy of remembering it. Back in the '70s, the definition of terrorism was greatly expanded far beyond engaging in it, directly supporting it, and financing it. First it was expanded to those who supported terrorism ideologically, then it became those, according to the government, who likely supported it, though no proof had to be provided, then it became anyone the government didn't like. That's been the definition ever since T. Wilson became president. Terrorism by Faithers is nil. Terrorism by Anarchists surpassed those by Muslims and CHIN sympathizers back in the '80s. You all don't know anything about anything.

"For the duration of our time together, I don't want to hear a word from any of you. Not one world. You people are certifiable. The second we get to the compound I'm going to ask to be separated from you, because if I were them, I wouldn't take you back." Stein moves to the driver's compartment. "I truly don't know why you are here. You people are the most morose, negative, sorry sacks of life I have ever encountered. They offer you a way back in and this is how you act." Stein sits in his chair and sees the

SUV in front of him with very bright rear lights. "Sit down! Or jump out! I don't care which. We're driving."

China
7:01 a.m., 26 October 2096

The jungle surrounds the tiny, ancient city, but the tree-shaded roads are modern and fairly new, courtesy of the government. A convoy of several cars are parked to the side of the road. A female soldier in a black uniform stands at the rear passenger side of the lead limo. The window rolls down and a middle-aged man speaks to her.

"Call in the troops. We will move within the hour."

"The dissidents, commander?" she asks.

"The Underground Church."

"They still exist, commander?"

"Of course. They've been hiding for a long time, but their flaw is that they must always come together to worship their false gods. We are not the Americans who let them live. Or the Russians who just exile them. We will terminate all of them. If fifty percent of the population are members or collaborators, then we kill fifty percent. It is why Great China is strong and will eventually inherit the earth."

"Yes, commander. This is the most amazing news we have ever heard. The woman stands to attention and is almost crying." She salutes him. "I am so honored to work under you, commander. After our president, you are the greatest man to ever live."

The man smiles. "You are a good soldier. You will be rewarded for your service and dedication. Call in the order."

"Yes, commander."

The woman runs back to her waiting black military vehicle behind his armored limo. She gets into the passenger side.

The window rolls back up. Inside the commander leans forward in his seat, about to say something to the driver. *The SUV explodes!*

The female soldier and the male soldier in the driver's seat sit motionless. A smirk appears on her face.

Trog-land, America
12:03 a.m., 26 October 2096

The convoy follows the lighted vehicle for hours. They don't know where they are going and there seems to be no end in sight. Stein is exhausted, but after the chewing out he gave everyone, he doesn't ask anyone to relieve him. Most of them are asleep anyway and no one is sitting in the driver compartment with him.

The steering wheel locks.

"We're here," Stein calls out.

The auto-drive takes control of the RV and instead of slowing down, speeds up. Everyone looks out the windows and one of them adjusts the controls to day-sight—night, but makes it look like daytime. They see nothing that indicates civilization, only wasteland.

"They'll probably drive us around for another four hours," one of them says.

Stein sighs and reclines the driver's seat back. He closes his eyes to sleep.

Murabba Presidential Palace, Riyadh, Saudi Arabia
11:49 a.m., 26 October 2096

The Emperor stares coldly at the men assembled before him. A bodyguard stands on either side of him, seated in his royal chair behind the desk.

"We think they have it, Supreme Excellency," one man says.

The look on the Emperor's face simmers with rage.

"Please don't kill us, Supreme Excellency. Let us redeem ourselves. We will find them."

"You tell me that the Apostates have seized not one, not five, but thirty weapon transports," the Emperor says. "Enough for them to be to a real army, an army against the Caliphate, and you grovel before me to talk of redemption."

"Excellency, this I-R-A will never get to use one of those weapons against the Empire."

"Supreme Excellency, may I put forth the idea that this I-R-A did not do this alone," another man says.

"Who?"

"The Americans, the CHINs, the Kurdish Separatists, Jews, Crusaders. Their treachery knows no bounds. Allah has many enemies. This I-R-A surely did not accomplish this feat alone. We must find and destroy their conspirators too."

"Interesting how all this is happening after the American president's announcement of the Sphere Program," the Emperor says.

Trog-land, America
7:23 a.m., 26 October 2096

Stein remembers waking up. He remembers the RV doors opening and Elliott waiting outside to greet them with another Goth-looking woman—probably Goth Lila. He has a faint memory of Pagan Paul with his stupid silver helmet. And then there was the stern-looking Asian man standing next to him.

Stein closes his eyes again and holds his temples with his hands.

"They drugged us," a voice says.

He can tell it's a particularly annoying Exile sitting next to him. He opens his eyes and they are all standing outside near a double dome-like structure, about five stories high. All around him are his fellow Exiles, in the same gray jumpsuits—he can't remember when they changed clothes.

From the side of the structure someone drives towards them in a golf cart—a common mode of transportation in enclaves. It is the same Asian man that was with Pagan Paul at their arrival. He is dressed in a black suit and they can see the outline of some tattoo at his neckline, a glimpse of his body tattoo.

He steps out of the cart, stands before them, and bows. He rises back up to address them.

Someone in the crowd breaks protocol. "I'd like to ask a question, before we officially get started," a sour-faced man says. "It is about the governmental structure of your enclave communities. We've been told they are secular, but I don't know if we believe that. Are they not actually quasi-theocracies?"

"If a government is only made up of the religious, then it is by definition a theocracy? Is that your definition of the word?"

"No, but—"

"Only the irreligious can run government?"

"No, I don't believe—"

"Why are you here then? Why do you wish to leave a world run by the irreligious you love for the religious you hate?"

"I don't hate anyone. And the irreligious you refer to are not atheists. They're Pagans. That's what we call them in America. Anti-religious, militant bigots. That's not atheists in the main. Their world is an *atheocracy*, to create a new word. A theocracy of militant atheists. We don't like that either."

"Faith World's government is civilian, pluralistic, and secular, run for the mutual protection of all the peoples of the Continuum. No religion, or lack thereof, is supreme. Theocracy in Judaism and Christianity almost destroyed them. Old Shinto Buddhism was wiped out because of it. Caliphate Islam will inevitably die because of theirs."

The Asian man walks to the man and slaps him. The man holds his face with a stunned look as the Yakuzu man glares at him.

"That is not for your question, but the impudence in speaking without permission." He turns from him to take his position in front of all the Exiles. "You may address me as Mr. Yang. Maybe one day you will have the distinction to know my real name. I do not care about your name. You have chosen to return to your people despite your dishonor. You dare call yourself Jew or Christian, despite your excommunication. Your God has seen fit to give you a second chance on this earth, for if it were up to Man, you would be left to die the deaths you deserve.

"This is your new home, for as long as we deem necessary. You will be judged based on your behavior, your actions, and your obedience from the moment you enter the structure. If you are deemed worthy of redemption and reunification, I will appear behind you. I will strike you to the ground and you will fall. I will offer my hand and pick you up. I will offer my hand in friendship and give you a white uniform to replace the disgusting gray one— the mark of your dishonor—that you wear now. You will be transported to Faith World and your life reborn will begin. All your past will never be spoken of again because that person and that life will have never existed.

"I outline the best scenario that could happen to you. If you make it, you will be turned over to Mr. Ying—the one you know as Pagan Paul. Mostly likely, however, there will be two other possibilities. The first likely possibility is that you will be left here. One day, myself, my staff, those deemed worthy will be gone. You will have been deemed unworthy. It will be your responsibility to make your way back to whatever metropolis you can find. It will be your responsibility to survive the trek, the elements, and Trogland. You will most assuredly die. For that reason in your disgusting gray outfit in your outside right pocket is a pill of poison. Though Faithers frown on suicide and some expressly forbid it, you are such a fallen being that the normal rules that apply to people and animals do not apply to you. Your dishonor has rendered you such.

"The second likely possibility,"—Mr. Yang pulls a laser pistol from inside his suit jacket—"is that you will die right now."

The Exiles freeze.

"I will ask only one question. If it doesn't apply, begin walking to the structure, enter through the door, and your assessment begins. If you do so, but lie, I will shoot you dead. If it applies, you must stand where you are. Questions?"

The look on everyone's faces is of fear and nervousness.

A woman raises her hand slowly. "May I ask why we are being given a second chance? May I ask that?"

Mr. Yang ignores her. "We begin. My question: are you collaborating with the government?"

No one moves at first—everyone looks at one another.

"We all collaborated with the government," a male Exile says. "When? You have to tell us up until when."

Yang watches them quietly without moving, without answering.

"You have to be clear. I'm not going to…we're not going to risk our lives on trick questions."

"Just stop it," Stein yells. "It isn't a trick question. It is very clear. The answer is none of us can move. None of us are walking through the front door. We all did. The question does not indicate a when."

"Look at the lawyer brain work," a female Exile says. "Says you.

Lawyers can't agree on the color of the sky. Why should we listen to you? Risk our lives based on what you say? You're probably a mole to get us killed."

Another man steps forward. "The question is moot. None of us collaborated. We were following the law! I'm tired of being called a collaborator and those Wolf Packers calling me a quisling in German. None of us collaborated. We were following the law. The government tells us to report people and places of worship who were using unsanctioned Torahs and Bibles—not using sanctioned Good Bibles, then we did it. We had to register with the government to work, to live our lives in the cities. Nothing wrong with that. I wasn't ashamed of my faith. I didn't care who knew about it. None of us collaborated. That's the trick of his question. Do we believe we were collaborators? The answer is no. Or, at least, I wasn't."

The man starts walking defiantly towards the structure. Soon others follow. Stein remains where he is, as do others. He realizes that half are walking to the structure and half are remaining behind. He feels nauseous and closes his eyes, and his legs feel wobbly. *Half of them are going to die!*

He hears the sounds. Most laser pistols are virtually silent, but others are purposely made to pop, more so for the wielder to know they fired. He opens his eyes slowly and, in the distance, he can see all the bodies cut down, lying on the ground. He looks at the others near him, their faces red, eyes red, tears streaming down some faces. They are all frozen like statues, not moving an inch.

This is real. It's all very real. The death is real!

Stein manages to look in the direction of Mr. Yang, but he is walking away from them.

"There is no buying your way back in," Yang says. "We will interrogate you and our mind-benders are not part psychologists.

They are part exterminators. We determine if you are a spy beyond what you have already done. If so, we will kill you."

Yang continues to walk away until he reaches the door of the structure, passing through the bodies on the ground, and disappears inside. They all hear a noise behind them, but are afraid to look. A long multi-seater trolley drives up and stops in front of them. A lone woman sits in the driver's compartment. She stands and motions everyone onto the trolley. Everyone slowly gets on and sits, the seats facing towards the back.

Elliott did warn them—Faithers will do anything to ensure the protection of their people and their enclaves. Anything. The Grid-government instigated religious civil wars, the Fall of Jewish Israel, the Registration Initiatives, Project Purify, the reign of President T. Wilson. "Turn-the-other cheek" Faithers no longer exist in the world. Stein tries to hold his panic at bay. There is no way back now.

As the trolley does a 180-degree turn to drive the way it came, they can see the structure grow smaller and smaller as they drive away. The bodies are not visible anymore, but it is all they can think of. He imagines the cushy and happy reception the Hiddens and Lots will be given. But this is theirs. There is a sudden drop—the trolley is driving down into the ground. Down they go. All Stein can feel is the sense that they are going down to a dark Hell to be interrogated, tortured, and buried alive.

Metro Hub, Outer San Diego, America
5:33 a.m., 26 October 2096

Drones hover in the sky and storm trooper law enforcement patrol the area. To most, they instill a sense of security, but he isn't an average member of the public.

He doesn't enter the depot station with his one small suitcase, but walks around the perimeter of the building, all the way around to the rear to the outside Outlands Bus Station. Here one buys passage to go to any number of outer-tek-city stops. Tek-cities are sophisticated and urban; Outlands are rural and low-tek.

He sees his snake-bus, or at least, that's what everyone calls it; there must be a technical name—five buses linked together with the ability to bend around corners, but they are just as fast as any other auto-drive transportation, save the fast-track.

"ID," the bus attendant says to him.

The man hands him his national identification card with his picture. Five seven, brown hair, brown eyes, 180 pounds.

"Are my bags here?" the man asks.

"They are." The attendant puts the man's ID in his vest pocket. "Seat 43."

"Do I get that back?"

"Why? Do you plan to return?"

"It's a keepsake."

"Seat 43."

They stare at each other.

"Sir, they have trackers embedded in the cards."

"Which you can remove."

"Take it up with your elders when you arrive."

The man reluctantly boards the large bus, climbing up the stairs. The aisle seems to go back forever. People, already seated, watch him. He moves past the rows—men, women, children. At some point he stops making eye contact. He starts moving faster down the aisle and is relieved to finally see the number 43. He climbs in, but then jumps back up to check the overhead and under-chair compartments. All his suitcases are there. He sits back down.

He has never liked the terms. Hiddens are Faithers living in secret communities in the tek-cities. Lots looked like every other tek-dweller, hiding their religion, hiding in plain sight within the tek-cities. Six years ago, the Continuum repatriated a large group of Hiddens and Lots, but many, including him, did not take the Continuum up on its offer. But much can change in six years—like Russians dropping fission bombs on Faithers.

"What Order?" someone says, and he turns.

A silver-haired man is sitting in the adjacent seat across the aisle.

"Christian."

"Me too. Which sub-order?"

"Sub-order? Do they have sub-orders anymore?"

"You're right. No. All the Protestant Orders merging together. There was a time when there used to be thousands of different sub-orders. Kinda funny, don't you think? Christians merged into one and Jews have like a dozen sub-orders now."

"Yeah, I guess so. Family?"

The silver-haired man hesitates as his face grows sad. "Not anymore."

"I'm sorry."

"No, it's okay. Not your fault or mine."

"I'm reuniting with mine. We haven't seen each other for many years, but we kept in contact. They finally convinced me." He can see the man is not listening. "I'm sorry you have to leave family behind."

"They hate me, so this final separation is okay by me. The only thing they didn't do is turn me in. That's the only favor they ever granted me. So I had to tolerate the hate."

"We leave all that behind."

"Well, we're not there yet."

The bus departs when the final passenger boards; four hundred people—about half are families. As soon as the snake-bus gets to the main freeway, its speed kicks in and quickly reaches almost one hundred miles an hour.

The bus is driving itself with the bus attendant sitting in a middle seat at a front console, which rose from the floor as soon as he secured the side door and sat in his chair. To those passengers immediately behind him, the console display is blank, but the attendant is wearing clear glasses to see the virtual screen.

A man sitting in the front seat gets up, steps forward, and crouches down near the attendant.

"Do we expect trouble?"

"Sir, please sit back in your seat with your family. We always expect trouble, even when we don't expect it."

The man returns to his seat with his wife and daughter.

"I hate this," he says to her. "This is why we never did this before. I feel like a criminal. It's like we're going off to a leper colony."

"What's a leper colony, Father?" the daughter asks.

"I'll tell you later."

"We talked about this for over a year," the wife says. "We want her raised in the faith."

"Don't put me in this," the daughter snaps. "I don't want to go. I'm okay with hiding. It's easy. Just don't say God or Jesus or Bible or Torah or any religious words. How is that hard?"

"You'll understand when you're older," her mother says.

"I am old enough. You have to turn everything into some big drama."

"Big drama? Is that what you think? Your father and I are tired of fighting with you. At least now we'll have an entire enclave to help us. We need that support, desperately. When you turn 18 you can go back to the tek-city you love so much, where they call you names for doing nothing more than existing."

"Maybe," her father says, "you'll return in time for them to try to put you in a concentration camp like they tried before. Or a leper colony. Can you figure out what that is now?"

The daughter covers her ears with her hands, upset.

A half-hour later, the bus attendant speaks into his mic-wand. "Attention. We are arriving. Follow the procedures you rehearsed in your exercises."

The snake-bus crosses the freeway threshold leaving the official tek-city behind and into the encircling outskirts of the Outlands. Most have seen it already, but they all look out the snake-bus's large windows. The buildings are far smaller and spread out, fewer visible signs of tek, no drones in the air, and large areas of dirt, brush, and nothing.

Who lives here? they think.

The passengers in the front seats notice there is not one car on their road. The bus barrels forward.

"Where are all the cars?" one of them asks.

"Oh my God," one of them calls out. The woman stands up from her seat causing panic among those who see and hear her.

People also start to see the flashing red and blue lights—the police! The bus slows to a stop, ten feet away are a half dozen police cars. The door of the bus opens and the bus attendant exits. Stormtroopers—police clad in black body-armored uniforms—are exiting their police cars and approaching.

The bus attendant has his ID ready as two storm troopers reach him and stop.

"Hello, sir. Where might this bus be going?"

"We're taking a sight-seeing tour to see the Outlands and surrounding area."

"You're taking them into Trog-land?"

"No, of course not. Just to take a peek beyond the perimeter."

"You're going to have to return to your transport, turn around, and go back the way you came. A new directive has gone into effect. You need a special pass to leave the city."

"This is the Outlands."

"Which is now under the jurisdiction of the city."

"When did this take effect?"

"This week, which is why we're giving you a courtesy warning rather than a ticket or performing an arrest."

"Okay. Then thanks for that."

"Wait!" another stormtrooper yells, running to them.

Unknown Location, Wastelands
5:00 a.m., 26 October 2096

A giant hangar rises from the ground, revealing the entrance. Dozens of civilian soldiers all wearing some type of cowboy hat and dressed in uniforms of all black, navy, deep crimson red, and browns enter the giant hangar. Jewish Order members have Star of Davids on their hats or on the center of their chest. Catholics all wear a collar around their necks. Protestants have crosses on their hats or on the center of their chest. Mormons have double cross symbols on their sleeves. Shinto members wear deep crimson uniforms with the cursive crosses across the chest of their uniform and the ancient Japanese-style cowboy hats of the historical shogun. In the center, the Cowboy Rabbi (Yonah) leads them in as he pulls on his leather gloves tight. His shiny pistols in their double holsters are intermittently visible as his long coat flaps open as he moves.

Outlands, San Diego
6:55 a.m., 26 October 2096

"We didn't know anything about this new law," the bus attendant says to three stormtrooper police. "We'll turn the bus around and drive back."

A policeman is listening to his ear-set and holds up his hand, index finger pointed in the air, gesturing the attendant to wait. The policeman says to the voice from his ear-set. "Yes, understood." The indicator light on the side of his helmet disconnects. "Sir, we're going to have to ask for all your passengers to disembark and form a single line in front of the bus."

"Why? We're not doing anything. We're on a sight-seeing trip."

"Please comply with our instructions, sir. More police are on the way."

"Are we being arrested?"

"You will all be taken in for questioning."

The attendant shakes his head. "Why are you doing this? This new law was never publicly announced."

"Ignorance of the law is not a defense for not following it, sir."

"If you don't comply, we will have to arrest you and everyone else, and seize the bus and all the possessions on it," another trooper says.

The attendant is visibly upset but says nothing and walks back to the bus.

Then another trooper talks into his ear-set. "We believe we have a whole bus load of them. Multiple positives from surveillance. Yes, sir, multiple units are already en route."

Several drones appear in the sky and take up positions above the snake-bus.

The attendant gets on the bus and reluctantly grabs the microphone wand from his driver compartment. The front passengers notice a globe drone descend and watch him through the open door.

The entire bus is in a panic, people standing from their seats, looking out the windows at the arriving police cars and more drones in the sky.

"What's happening?" someone asks.

"I apologize everyone, but we're going to have to get off the bus and line up in front."

"Why?" a man asks.

"They claim there is a new law that no one can leave the tek-city without city permission."

"I want to talk to someone in authority," a male passenger calls out. "We're citizens. We have rights!" The man moves from his seat and begins walking to the front of the bus. His wife and son try to restrain him. "No. They will continue to do this until we stand up to them."

"Please, sir, let's not cause problems," the attendant says.

"You were supposed to guarantee our safety." The man points at him. "My family is on this bus."

The attendant blocks his way out of the bus. "Do not do anything. This isn't about you or your family. This is about everyone on this bus. Everyone, please, let's calmly get off. Everything will be fine. Trust me."

In moments, everyone is lined up outside the bus as troopers board to search it while others watch the passengers.

The attendant's ear-set rings. He walks to the lead stormtrooper. "This call is for you."

"Who is it?"

"Our lawyer."

He smiles. "Have them call 911."

"You cannot detain us like this."

"Actually, we can. Get back into line, sir, or we will have to handcuff you."

"You really need to take this call."

"Are you refusing to comply, sir?"

The attendant touches his ear-set. "They won't take the call, Mr. Elliott." He listens. "They're threatening me with restraint." He disconnects the call and goes back to his spot in the line.

The lead trooper's ear-set begins to ring. He looks at his two fellow officers. "Answer," he says.

"Hello," a voice says.

"Who is this?" the stormtrooper asks.

"This is Elliott Finegold, officer," the voice says. "You are to release these civilians immediately."

"How did you get this number? Use of a law enforcement channel by unauthorized person is illegal."

"I'm trying to be civil. Is this how you want to proceed?"

"We don't need your permission."

"We will not allow you to take our people."

"Is that so?"

The line disconnects. The lead trooper gives a signal to his men and they draw their weapons. "Arrest all of them," he says.

"Look!" A stormtrooper points to the sky.

A tracer missile arcs down to them. As they run one way to the bus for cover, the bus attendant gives the signal and the passengers run en masse in the opposite direction farther into the Outlands. The troopers dive for cover as the mini missile crashes near them, but there is no explosion.

The troopers get to their feet.

"They're getting away," one of them says. "Should we engage?"

"No, forget them. I'm ordering a retreat until military back-up can get here."

"But we've been ordered to arrest them, not let them get away."

"A bunch of families with children won't get very far."

"I once saw a seven-year-old terrorist blow a soldiers brains out."

"I guess we know who's aiming for a promotion."

The trooper is offended. "How do you know this wasn't part of their plot to attack us?"

"They didn't know we'd be here."

"What's wrong with you? They fired missiles at us! They were ready for us."

"All the more reason to withdraw until reinforcements arrive!"

"We don't need back-up to capture a bunch of Jew-Christians. And they can't drop missiles on us if we have them in gun-sight or have them, period. We're supposed to be the elite police. There was a time when police were able to capture and kill criminals without any drone support or advanced body armor or reinforcements. It was done all the time. Tek makes some people soft. Do you need the little machines to hold it for you when you go to the bathroom?"

"Get out of my face."

"Do what you want. We're following District orders and apprehending the terrorist fugitives."

The man gestures and he leads six of the troopers—two of them in heavy robot suits—after the fleeing passengers, leaving the rest of the stormtrooper force behind.

The passengers run through the wooded area. Ahead, they see a man approaching wearing black with a long flapping coat, leather gloves on his hands, and shiny pistols in double holsters.

"Keep going," he yells, directing them to run past him. "Get over the ridge. The rescue transports are waiting."

"But our things," a woman yells. "My family's things. I have heirlooms that barely survived the Holocaust." She stops running and looks back to the snake-bus behind her.

"Hey, Lot's wife!" Yohan yells.

The Biblical reference makes the woman look at him.

"*People* are more important than things."

She stops herself and continues running with the rest of the passengers.

Everyone passes him and disappear over the hill. The chasing stormtroopers quickly approach.

"Stop there!" one yells. "Put your hands in the air!"

"Go back where you came from," Yonah says, angrily. "They're unarmed families!"

"I will shoot you dead if your hands are not in the air."

The Cowboy Rabbi draws his guns and fires so fast that none of the troopers can react. Six men shot in the forehead—four collapse to the ground and the two troopers in robot suits fall back with a large thud.

"I gave you your chance not to be a Nazi."

Three mortars land and blanket the entire area around the bus not with explosions, but opaque smoke. The stormtroopers, their transports, and the bus are engulfed. Drones arrive, but are instantly all shot from the sky by multiple high-powered rounds— a few explode, most just crash to the ground.

A dozen hovercraft appear, firing laser tracer rounds into the smoke. More mortar rounds arc over the sky-craft from multiple locations crashing into the center of the smoke with the concussion rounds exploding in increasing intensity. The firing stops as the hovercraft land. Different drones fly out from the top of the craft and blow the remaining smoke away to reveal stormtrooper bodies lying everywhere unconscious and their vehicles destroyed. The snake-bus is untouched. Cowboy Coalition members, with weapons drawn, race into the scene.

"What do you want done?" Lariat asks. His face is masked with black opaque goggles.

The Cowboy Rabbi surveys the scene, his face also masked with goggles. "I'm tempted to make an example of them."

"It could be something simple, but still makes the point," Runningstar says.

"I'm tempted, but I've never been one to kick someone when they're already down and unconscious. Defeats the purpose."

"Their weapons and comms?" Lariat asks.

"Leave them. Nothing they have is better than our tek. We have what we want. Leave the incendiaries and let's go."

In moments, every Cowboy is back on their hovercraft and in the air. The bombs explode reducing the remnants of the destroyed police vehicles to burning liquefied metal. The three rear sky-craft launch a volley of missiles as the entire air convoy jets forward faster than sound.

A swarm of globe drones approach the Outlands' scene. The missiles strike and the explosions send every drone crashing to the ground.

Inside the lead hovercraft, Cowboy Coalition members cheer.

"In, touchdown, total destruction, rescue, and back up in the air, gone in less than five minutes!" says one member.

"Four minutes, thirty-six seconds!" corrects another.

Yohan is in the corner of the command room by himself with a comm-phone to his ear for semi-privacy. "The stormtroopers were waiting for them," he says. "They tried to make it look like it was a random stop, but they were waiting."

The hover transports fly across the Wastelands. The passengers are all clustered around the nearest window watching everything as the craft sets down.

"Everyone, please exit as quickly as possible," one of the new drivers commands, appearing from the cockpit. "Hurry!"

They jump out of multiple exits and their shoes touch the hot, barren soil. There is nothing anywhere around them as far as they can see. The five drivers join them and can see the unease in the passenger's faces.

One of the driver's points. "There!"

Four separate roto-planes appear and glide to them. The sky-ships engage their rotors to hover and then set down 15 feet away from the crowd. People exit and quickly move to them.

"Hello," a woman holds up her tablet. "Jewish Order."

"Christian Order," another says.

"Everyone, the initial bus was recovered," a driver calls out. "Your belongings will be waiting for you at your destination."

"Catholic Order, here."

"All for the Gnostic Order, here."

There are smiles, some muffled cheers, as the crowds break into smaller groups to follow their designees back to one of the roto-jets.

One of the men stops and walks back to the five drivers.

"Yes, sir?" one of them asks.

"The stormtroopers knew we were there."

"Sir, don't worry about those things. Get on your plane and enjoy the flight. You'll be at your new home soon."

"But—"

"Sir," says another driver. "We know what you know. And more. Don't worry yourself about it. The Continuum will take care of it. We'll never allow anything to jeopardize Faith World."

One of the drivers points to the roto-jets. "They will fly off and leave you here."

The man's neck whips around and he runs. The man is pulled onto his craft and the doors close. The roto-jets start to rise into the air.

"I bet you it was him," says another driver.

"We know no such thing. He could become one of your neighbors, for all you know.

"I'll move then. Until I know they're all cleared. Where do you think the government has all their spies? With the Exiles or with these?"

"Everyone must get the benefit of the doubt. Stop trying to spoil a beautiful day. Now how about our new Cowboy Coalition?"

"All my kids want to be Cowboys."

"Kids? Forget the kids. I want to be a Cowboy."

"I thought you wanted to join the Jewish Wolf-Pack or the Shinto so you'd get a samurai sword."

"I want to do all of it."

Murabba Presidential Palace, Riyadh, Saudi Arabia
4:46 p.m., 26 October 2096

A sheik angrily recites the reports. "They are saying that this Igor's bomb, as they are calling it, was a religious plot to destabilize the region. They are trying to spread lies that the Supreme Caliphate was behind it. Lies, all of it!"

The Emperor calmly says, "The greatest mass murderers of the last century and this one were godless atheist infidels, but they continue to lie about Islam."

"Emperor, I implore you not to join with the infidels in their

Sphere Program. It is nothing but a plot against the Caliphate."

"I have no intention of doing so. But we can create our own."

Zhongnanhai Presidential Palace, Beijing, China
7:02 p.m., 26 October 2096

The Deputy says, "He was killed by a remote-detonated car bomb."

"He was in charge of finding all the ring leaders of the Underground Church, correct?" President Wen asks.

"Yes, President, it must have been them."

"Or someone who wants us to think it was them. Maybe it was you?"

The man smiles. "President, I would never. I never allow my own ambitions to supersede the State."

"I want the perpetrators."

"We will find them, President. We always do."

The White House, America
10:01 p.m., 26 October 2096

"We're getting conflicting reports that the Brazilian president and his family fled the country or were imprisoned. There are other conflicting stories that they escaped to Australia or were killed. We haven't been able to confirm if the entire military command staff was executed. We have been able to confirm that the country's former communications secretary appointed himself the new president. A man by the name of Khan."

The president sits quietly as the staffers debrief him. He is weary from an endless day of briefings and meetings.

"No one saw this coming, sir," says another staffer. "His forces are expelling all diplomats from the county, but they are also burning our American embassy and seizing all American holdings."

President looks at Homeland and his senior advisors

"Sir, it's coming over the news feed," says another. "The new Brazilian president has declared Brazil the fourth global superpower and is threatening all of the Spanish Americas."

"And there is news in Mexico, sir."

President T. Wilson waits for it.

"The Mexican president lost his election. The new president might be—"

"A Jew-Christian."

"We're not sure, sir. He could be simply a sympathizer. But don't worry. He won, but a strong anti-religious, secular bloc opposed him. They're protesting in the streets now saying his election is illegal."

"Please leave us for a moment," the president says.

The men rise from their seats and exit the Oval Office leaving the Homeland Director and the two senior advisors behind. The door closes.

"Is there more?" he asks Homeland.

The Director of Homeland Defense and Intelligence Agency has dark eyes and short blonde hair angled into her chin.

"This new Brazilian president has also severed ties with Canada," she answers.

"He knows," a senior advisor says.

"He can't possibly know," the other says.

"We also believe he's organizing his own secret summit with the CHINs and the Caliphate. We haven't been contacted," Homeland adds.

The president leans back in his chair. The anger simmers within.

"We've lost our entire North American buffer zone on the

northern and southern borders in a day. Decades of painstaking work gone—in an instant." The president stands and stares out the bay window. "We must assume they know. Clear my calendar of everything and get Garrison in here. We're officially abandoning the Buffer Zone and moving forward with the back-up contingency."

"They wouldn't dare attack us, sir," Homeland says.

"Why? We can barely fight a two-front war, but a three-front war? I would attack America if I were them. We all tried to do it to the Russian Bloc."

"Back-up contingency, sir? Reinstatement of the draft?" one senior advisor asks.

"Don't be absurd."

"No, Mr. President."

"What kind of military do you think we'd have infested with sex-fiends, drug-fiends, VR-fiends. We already have a forced attrition rate on nearly twenty-five percent now. The Caliphate and the CHINs armies are free of all of that. No, the back-up contingency plan it is."

"Sir, is this all connected with that terrorist call you received?" Homeland asks.

"Why do you ask that?"

"We did indirectly align with them against the Internationalists, along with the Muslims and CHINs. They were so successful that even we don't know how they did it. These Jew-Christians have global capabilities and there's no point pretending they're Luddites living out in the middle of desert wastelands."

He looks at her coldly. "I have *never* thought that. To create the American empire I wanted, to assemble the power I needed, it always meant destroying them. I knew that forty years ago. I also knew that—to use a late friend's words—would cause them to *evolve*. And they have. I accept the fact that I've created my own archenemies that possibly we'll never be able to fully destroy now, but they don't live here anymore. I am the President of the United States and they aren't. We control the nation—now and forever. Religion in America is a distant memory to the people, so I'm content with all my decisions and actions. "

"How do you want to proceed now, sir?" the Homeland Director asks.

"I want the Sphere Program accelerated. We'll go it alone."

"Then other superpowers will do the same, sir," the other advisor adds. "From outside the program they'll view it as 'weaponizing' cities, not 'futurizing' them. Exactly what we wanted to prevent."

The president pays no attention to him. "I wonder. Who is running the bigger conspiracy? There are so many."

"Sir, you don't think the terrorist was being truthful?" Homeland asks. "That they can read our minds?"

"My mind," the president corrects. "It doesn't matter. I've already handled it."

"What is the back-up contingency plan then, sir?" an advisor asks. "I'm not familiar with it."

"If our North American buffer zone that we've been working on for decades is gone, then we need to immediately begin building a new army, separate from our robotics and biologics war divisions. War-robots and man-made life forms fill two of our three battlefield needs; we require a human army too. And since we don't have enough humans, we'll grow them—a clone army. Five million, ten million, fifty million. However many subjects we need to match the Caliphate, and especially the CHINs—whatever it takes."

"But wasn't your late national campaign manager, Lucifer

Mestopheles, going to be the template? We purged all his DNA from the stocks. But yes, with an executive order we can access the Registry, access to all the genetic material in the nation. Who would the replacement material come from, sir?" Homeland asks.

President T. Wilson sits back in his chair. "Me."

*The After Eden Series: **Pure Conspiracy***
continues in ***Red Halo*** (Book #4).

...twenty-nine years later.

Transmission Intercept #114790 (World War III)

[Date tag: 13 September 2125] Rube, please respond. I'll keep resending. Pro-Caliphate Muslims have seized the Canadian government, no doubt triggered by the Caliphate attack on New York City. Canada has erupted in civil war. The Quebecois are fighting Muslim forces in the East, and all sects of the Star Trek have joined with Jedis to fight the Muslims in the West. Not a single Canadian soldier has yet responded to Caliphate invasion forces. Sources say the Canadian military has instead taken up fortified positions on the border to protect America. Sources also say that the Canadian president and his entire Cabinet have already fled the country. {Unintelligible expletives; not English} It burst on the Net—Russian Bloc forces have invaded! That means they're either completely ignoring their Witch Wars or have already dealt with it. Canada can't stop the Russian Bloc military, so this isn't to invade Canada, but America! Rube, I have to go now; it's total chaos in-country. I hear gunfire and mortar explosions, and I see fire, smoke, and looting everywhere around me. Rube, get as far away from America as possible. This is it. This must be World War III. See you at checkpoint Charlie. Live long and prosper.

Department of Homeland Defense and Intelligence Agency Security Dispatch / 13 September 2125

Sender is identified as Lorian Denak, a journalist of Vulcan, Alberta, Canada. Recipient (called "Rube") has been identified as anti-American journalist and activist named Sprocket. Canada has fallen and the entire Canadian government has fled the country for America. Confirmed: Russian Bloc military invaded Canada at

00:10 hours. Threat Matrix projects that Muslim forces now in control of Canada will fall to the Russians within the hour. Russian Bloc invasion of America via the northwestern states is imminent. No additional military forces will be redeployed to the northern border. All American military forces are committed to the battlefront against the Caliphate's Northeastern Atlantic invasion (designated: War of the Three Towers or "Wolf 359"). Threat Matrix predicts that PERFECT STORM Scenario is a ninety-percent probability, with projected attacks from CHIN forces via the Pacific and Brazilian forces from the southern border. If projections become reality, POTUS will formally declare the commencement of World War III.

Thank you for reading!

Dear Reader,

I hope you enjoyed *Pure Conspiracy*.

<u>Can You Write Me a Review?</u>

If you enjoyed ***Pure Conspiracy*** **(An *After Eden* Select Novel)**, I'd greatly appreciate a review on one or more of the following sites:

Reviews are the best way for readers to discover good books. My writer's motto is simple: "Readers Rule!" Thanks so much.

Always writing,

Austin Dragon

CONTINUE THE ADVENTURE

Get Your Next *After Eden* Book!

The After Eden Series (Chronological Order)

Thy Kingdom Fall (After Eden Series, Book #1)
Stars and Scorpions (After Eden Series, Book #2)
Metal Flesh (After Eden Series: Tek-Fall, Episode I)
Hell's Menagerie (After Eden Series: Tek-Fall, Episode II)
Rising Leviathan (After Eden Series, Book #3)
Pure Conspiracy (After Eden Select Novel)
Red Halo (After Eden Series, Book #4) Coming Soon!

The After Eden Series (Group Order)

Main After Eden Series
Thy Kingdom Fall (After Eden Series, Book #1)
Stars and Scorpions (After Eden Series, Book #2)
Rising Leviathan (After Eden Series, Book #3)
Red Halo (After Eden Series, Book #4) Coming Soon!

After Eden: Tek-Fall Companion Novels
Metal Flesh (After Eden Series: Tek-Fall, Episode I)
Hell's Menagerie (After Eden Series: Tek-Fall, Episode II)

After Eden Select Novel
Pure Conspiracy (After Eden Select Novel)

<u>**Also by Austin Dragon**</u>

See all my books in science fiction, cyberpunk, mystery, horror, YA dystopia, and fantasy at: **http://www.austindragon.com/books-of-author-austin-dragon/**

ABOUT THE AUTHOR

Austin Dragon is author of the *After Eden* **Series**, including the *After Eden: Tek-Fall* mini-series, the classic *Sleepy Hollow Horrors*, and the upcoming cyberpunk detective series, *Liquid Cool*. He is a native New Yorker, but has called Los Angeles, California home for the last twenty years. Words to describe him, in no particular order: U.S. Army; English teacher; one-time resident of Paris; political junkie; movie buff; campaign manager and staffer of presidential and gubernatorial campaigns; Fortune 500 corporate recruiter; renaissance man; dreamer.

He is currently working on the next books in the *After Eden* Series, and new books and series in mystery, fantasy, YA dystopia, classic horror, and more science fiction!

Connect with Austin on social media at:

Website and blog:
http://www.austindragon.com

Twitter:
https://twitter.com/Austin_Dragon

Pinterest:
http://www.pinterest.com/austindragon

Google+:
https://google.com/+AustinDragonAuthor

Goodreads:
https://www.goodreads.com/ADragon